what nell dreams

a novella & stories

what nell dreams

a novella & stories

by
anne leigh parrish

acknowledgements

picture this— February 10, 2017, *New Pop Lit*

what nell dreams—February 18, 2017, *Squawk Back*

shelter—September 15, 2017, *New Pop Lit*

collector of sorrows—December 2, 2017, *Flash Fiction Magazine*

good boy—February 6, 2018, *Sand Hill Review*

here's why—May 6, 2016, *New Pop Lit*

the first time—February 12, 2018, *New Pop Lit*

he said, she said—June 27, 2018, *New Pop Lit*

moonlight on the bay—September 20, 2018, *O: JA&L (Open: Journal of Arts & Letters)*

yellow—August 31, 2018, *The Slag Review*

people like them—Issue 2, *Mark Literary Review*

i know you—*Grindstone 2019 Literary Anthology*

a wild feeling—February 11, 2020, *New Pop Lit*

first cut—January 1, 2020, *The Nonconformist Magazine*

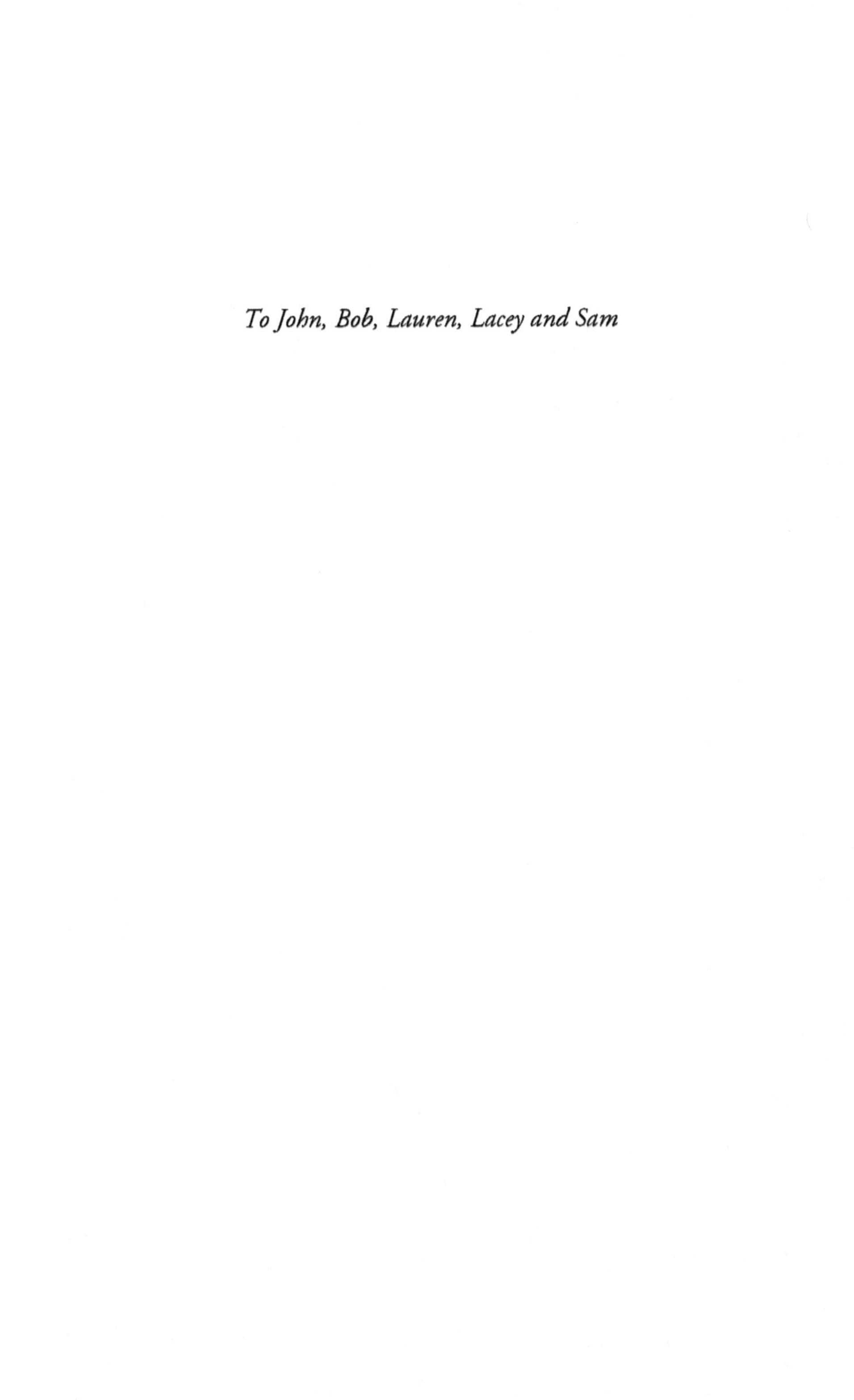

To John, Bob, Lauren, Lacey and Sam

table of contents

picture this

He wished she wouldn't block the light. If she had to stand before a window, why did it have to be the one he was trying to paint by? He explained—again—that this was the only window that faced north.

It was also the only one that gave the sea. Nina had to gaze at the waves. They filled her with joy.

Barth wasn't interested in her joy. He needed to unravel the truth of color and shape. What else really mattered? He was on to something big now; he could feel it. He'd felt it before, and never quite captured it, never made it truly his. That's why they were here, on this little turn of land, in a creaky house lent them by a very dear friend; so he could finally pin down what had eluded him for over ten years.

Poor Barth! All that frustration, all that perceived failure. The dear friend, Andy, was the one who kept his spirits afloat. Andy lived just down the road, in another creaky house. That he owned two homes in this remote corner of Maine's impossible coast was his ex-wife's doing. When their marriage frayed she said they should live apart, but near one another. Hence the two properties. He'd picked them both up for a song, one easy to sing on his income. Andy was an investment broker before the housing bubble burst. He got out in time, the wife moved back to Amherst, and left him with an empty house to fill.

"I took the money and ran like hell," he liked to say. He was 62, twenty years older than Barth. They'd met at the Y down in Portland, where Barth was teaching a painting class in an angry attempt to supplement their income. Andy sought to fill his leisure time with elegant pursuits.

Nina, aside from standing at the window and blocking Barth's light, worked part-time in an antiques store in the tiny town of Malverne, where people from Boston came for long weekends to get that particularly rustic Yankee charm only Maine could offer. The owner of the store, Dorothy Blackstock, was 84, widowed, cheerful, and foul-mouthed. Nina was 45, which meant nothing except that she was older than Barth, something which annoyed him in a way he could never articulate. Nina didn't swear, of which Dorothy disapproved.

Nina loved her job. She bought beautiful pieces for pennies on the dollar because Dorothy was only in business to keep herself amused. Her husband had left her a "little something", which Nina learned one day was a large sum. Dorothy had an office in a corner of the shop, and when she was seeing the dentist one morning, Nina tidied the papers on the charming drop front secretary she used as a desk. On top was a quarterly report from an investment company in New York stating that the combined value of Dorothy's mutual funds was just over four million dollars. Nina didn't know what the husband had done for a living. She'd assumed he'd been a fisherman, because that line of work went so well with the rocky landscape and abysmal weather.

In the four months they'd lived in the house, Nina had brought in a brass fire screen; a four-poster bed that groaned every time one of them turned over—never mind the racket when they actually made love, which wasn't often—a round table with an elegant inlay of circles and squares in a dark cherry tone; and a stunning ceramic pitcher on which a seascape had been hand-painted in blue. Barth called her a magpie, and said she was cluttering up the place. Another thing he insisted on besides sole ownership of the window was a Spartan environment, free of distractions.

"Can't you see that I'm trying to concentrate?" he asked.

"Oh, pooh."

She'd gotten good at humoring him. Maybe it was self-defense, given what she'd had to forgo. She'd been a guidance counselor at a high school in Portland. Young faces, bright eyes, all that energy and angst lit her up. She loved them all—each and every one. Was she compensating for having no children of her own? Maybe, but her lazy uterus had ultimately done her a favor, since Barth would have been a terrible father. The only thing he could nurture was his own sense of failure.

But that wasn't fair. There'd been years when he tried to comfort her when she couldn't conceive. He said two were a family, a good family at that. He'd grown up with three brothers and two sisters, a house full of noise and misery, hatred and resentment, never able to have his own space. That's why he became an artist—the lure of escape.

The escape became a trap. His ambition sucked all the pleasure from his work. He wanted recognition, praise, acclaim. Nina said he should look within himself for these things. Once he found them, the world would, too.

Her words angered him. She didn't understand. She wasn't an artist.

"True. But I know what it is to want something," she said.

She took care of everything. Groceries, cooking, cleaning, laundry, paying the bills, reminding him to take his vitamins, rubbing the knots out of his neck, taking his detailed list of paint supplies all the way down to Portland, a two-hour round trip, and waiting while the flaky teenage boy behind the counter found everything on it. She stopped at the bakery and bought him one of his favorite eclairs, although he'd declared that sugar was evil. As she expected, he ate it with delight.

Nina didn't have a cell phone. Barth said they caused brain cancer. The house had no telephone, either. Once a week she called her mother from Dorothy's store. Nina's mother lived in California. She wanted Nina to move there, too.

"That leech is bleeding you dry," her mother said.

Nina said she was happy with him.

"Liar."

"Mom."

"You're just putting a good face on things."

"Well, isn't that what people do?"

Nina's mother had endured Nina's father for decades until one day she said she'd had enough of long cold winters and followed the sun all the way west. She invited him to come, if he wanted to, but things were going to be strictly on her terms. He thought it over. He decided to stay in Maryland, where Nina had grown up. He'd gotten involved with a woman at the gym he went to. He thought he could make things work with her.

Beyond Nina's window a gull screeched. She watched it rise and fall over the surf. She longed suddenly for hollow bones.

"Everything's fine. I just called to check in," Nina said.

"Let me know when you're ready to check out. I'll even buy your ticket. You can be here tomorrow."

"Oh, Mom."

Then her mother had to go because she was meeting a neighbor for lunch, and later she was going to the symphony with a man whose cousin played first violin.

"There's a joke in there somewhere," Nina said.

"Oh, you. Take care of yourself. And tell what's-his-name to lighten up."

Dorothy returned from a second numbing trip to the dentist. The crown she'd had installed didn't fit properly. The dentist was a fucking idiot, in her opinion. A major douchebag, in fact.

Nina digested her slurred commentary. She despised Novocain, herself. She avoided the dentist by keeping her teeth and gums in excellent condition. She'd recently bought an electric toothbrush that emitted a high-pitched whine Barth couldn't tolerate, so she brushed over the kitchen sink, at the opposite end of the house from their bedroom.

Dorothy looked hard at Nina. She asked what was wrong.

"Nothing."

"Liah."

Nina just shook her head and dusted everything in sight.

That night the air was delightfully warm. The sand was smooth. And the surf! So mesmerizing to watch it rise and fall. The full moon bathed everything in the most delicious silver light.

In the morning, Nina checked her shoes. No sand. The calendar over the stove in the kitchen said the moon was in her first quarter.

Barth sat at his easel. Nina brought his coffee.

"Finally," he said.

"It only brews so fast."

"No. *That*." He pointed to the canvas. The painted scene was the one Nina had walked in the night before, the rocky shore replaced.

"You changed it," she said.

"Just now. The rocks were wrong."

They'd drawn him, in the beginning. He loved them because they were unforgiving. She was there, too, her back to him, facing the sea. She knew herself from the green sweater she always wore, and the long braid of red hair down her back.

"You don't like people in your pictures," she said.

"You're not people."

"An aardvark?"

"I mean you're a part of me."

"Just not a person."

"Why do you have to be like this, right when I'm having a breakthrough?"

She kissed the top of his head and left.

That night she lifted her arms to the full moon. She wasn't puzzled. She understood. She had learned to slide from one world to another, and that her presence in this other world was moving Barth forward. She was moved forward, too, because she could watch the waves for hours, learning their language, trusting their voice. And they trusted her, as well, though she never spoke a word.

At the store, Dorothy watched her over the top of bifocals. Nina flitted about with her feather duster. She caught Dorothy's gaze and stopped.

"What?" she asked.

"You made up."

"What do you mean?"

"You and that…*man* you live with."

"We didn't fight."

"No?"

"Of course not."

"Darling, forgive me, but you're full of shit."

Nina patted Dorothy on the shoulder. She was grateful for her spirited concern. She'd thought before that Barth might enjoy her company, if he'd ever consent to seeing anyone but Andy.

That evening Barth was elated. Everything was coming together.

"A woman watching the sea. What could be more evocative than that?" he asked.

"A man and a woman watching the sea."

Her comment didn't darken his mood. He'd been over to Andy's for a drink or two before Nina returned. Andy was excited by the turn of events. He thought there might be a collector he could talk to when the painting was done.

"And when will that be?" Nina asked.

"Any day now. I can *feel* it."

His reputation was made. *Return* hung in a Chelsea gallery only a couple of weeks before it caught the eye of a wealthy Frenchman. He understood it, he said. The woman, looking back over her shoulder with the smallest smile, if it were even a smile, more like an attitude, much like the Mona Lisa, no?

Barth agreed, though in that moment he couldn't recall the Mona Lisa. He could see only Nina. He decided at the last minute that she should glance behind her, so the viewer could see the hunger in her eyes. The hunger, though, was all in his. He accepted her departure now. At first, he hated her for abandoning him at a crucial moment. Then he despaired. He thought all the time about where she could have gone. She'd kept her plans to herself. Neither her mother nor Dorothy had had the slightest clue. They accused him of driving her away, or possibly even doing her in. The police had been all around the place. She'd taken nothing with her. No wallet, no clothes, not even her electric toothbrush. Did he have *any* idea where she might be? He had none. When they left, he stood at the window, willing the rocks to become sand, and for that sand to yield footprints.

what nell dreams

On Monday, it's about a horse. The eyes are remarkably kind, shy, even flirty under their thick veil of lashes. She looks at Nell from the side, sticking her large soft muzzle over the fence to nudge at her outstretched hand. That hand is empty—no sugar cube, apple, carrot, only the palm lines waiting for the mystic to decipher, dampened with sweat. The horse enjoys the salt of that sweat and licks it all away with one leisurely pass of its velvety tongue. Nell swoons with delight. *This is love, she thinks, this.*

Tuesday, her sister beats her with a riding crop. Monday's horse is hers. Nell is forbidden any contact. She is forbidden even to think of her. *You are not supposed to be here*, the sister says. *You are a mistake.* The crop is put down, and the sister uses her bare hands instead. When she tires of her abuse, the sister sits, exhausted, pitiable, needing love and attention. She receives none. Nor is she punished for her brutal acts. In Nell's dream world, she alone is punished.

Wednesday, the man she married fails her. He weeps with regret. His weakness becomes her strength, and she walks with him on her back through waving summer grass. His weight is great, yet lightens as she goes, until she can't feel him at all, pressing into her, clutching her shoulders and breathing on her neck. She meets a stream that flows joyously over smooth rocks, enhancing their gray color to a rich, dark blue. Nell is stunned by this sudden, unexpected beauty. When she turns her head to say, *Look! Won't you just look at this with me*, she finds that he's no longer there.

Thursday, the child she never had escapes from her womb in a rush of blood. The child is a boy with large blue eyes and a crooked grin. It wears a ring on its thumb engraved with stars. The stars are their point of origin, hers and the child's, and she removes the ring to wear it herself. She needs the stars to remain close to her, now that her body no longer contains them, but without the starred ring, the child wails painfully, losing its beauty, robbing her of the pleasure it gave her only moments before, so she returns the ring. Now starless, and unmoored, it is she who weeps.

Friday, she makes passionate, almost violent love with a man she's never met. She can't see his face, not because it's hidden, or there is no light, or her eyes are closed, but because she is so swept away by the energy of his almost painful thrusts that anything on which her gaze falls disappears. He continues his mounting rhythm until she has taken him all the way inside her, and there is nothing left of him beyond her. He is her blood, bone, and sinew. His flesh is hers. She wakes, bathed in sweat, with an ache in her teeth.

Saturday, she admires a tapestry hanging on a stone wall in a museum devoted exclusively to Medieval artifacts. She's amused by her outfit, a white mini-dress and white vinyl boots, in such a somber, dignified place. The image on the tapestry is of a unicorn standing in a circular fence, clearly captured, though the fence is low enough to jump over easily. Maybe it doesn't want to leave. Maybe it's humoring its captors, playing along, letting them feel in control. There's a look of whimsy in its woven eyes. As Nell leans in for a better look, the unicorn whispers, *Touch my horn, I beg you.* When Nell's finger brushes the wool, a single thread comes loose. She pulls and pulls, hand over hand, until the tapestry has unraveled into miles of red, gold, and green wool at her feet. She steps out of the pile, awed at her destruction. *Thank you*, comes a final whisper.

Sunday, flowers in her garden open in winter and snow falls in spring. The midday sky is littered with stars, and the sun burns at midnight. With this flouting of Time's law, she is cast adrift, excited to the point of giddiness as she rises through the roof, floating over trees and the fields beyond, until the land below is new, dotted with figures tending the earth lovingly, patting soil with such gentle hands she can feel their silky touch. Her flight continues until she knows she is about to lose her way entirely, that if she doesn't turn back now, she will never see home again. She pauses, hovering between past and future, savoring her freedom, wondering how she lived so long without it.

shelter

The party was at Jackson's place, at the end of an unpaved road, on the eastern tip of the island. In good weather it was a forty-five minute drive from town. The weather wasn't good. The rain had fallen for three days, sometimes turning lighter, even to a drizzle, but never once letting up.

People said Jackson was starting to lose it out there in that old shack he'd been renovating for the last nine months. When he tore the walls down to the studs, it had been spring. Now New Year's was barely behind them.

It was Susan's doing. She'd seen him in town and corralled him for a cup of coffee. She loved looking at his working man's hands around the mug he didn't drink from, as if its sole purpose was to provide warmth. She offered to handle everything—all the food and booze. She'd bring some tapes she'd just recorded of her all-girl bluegrass band, The Willows. At that, Jackson focused on his scarred thumb. Bluegrass wasn't really his thing.

Cara's truck bumped up the road, the rain in the headlights so thick it looked like snow. Drake was at the wheel. He insisted on driving. She was no good at it, he said, not on a road like this. Plus, the transmission was going. Hadn't she said she was going to get it fixed?

The edge in his voice matched the one in her heart. He'd been difficult lately. Regrets about choices made, paths not taken, had surfaced again. He admitted as much, and offered quick, curt apologies, then ran his hand through her hair. He didn't do that now, because the road required both on the wheel.

A darting deer caused him to swerve. He couldn't correct before sliding into the ditch.

"Shit!" he said.

"Shit's right."

"I didn't do it on purpose."

"Can you get out?"

The screaming spin of the tires said they were stuck.

It was only about another quarter of a mile. They'd have to go on foot. She'd dressed for the weather, he hadn't. He wore a natty sport coat that had belonged to his father, a tweed monster with suede patches on the elbows. He had a thing about his father, not a good thing, in Cara's opinion, because the guy was cold, harsh, and disconnected, all traits Drake readily agreed his father possessed, yet somehow longed to emulate. His jeans were new, bought off-island a few weeks before, along with the wingtips that made him slip with every other step. She offered to go ahead and see if someone at the house could drive back down and pick him up.

"It's too cold out here," he said.

"You could sit in the cab, with the heat on."

"Wastes gas."

"Well, come on, then."

Her boots had thick ridged soles that gripped the rocky wet surface. She slowed her pace to match his. He took her arm to keep from falling. They'd left the bottle of wine in the truck.

"Why didn't you remember?" he asked.

"Why didn't you?"

"You were the one who suggested bringing it."

"So what?"

The wind was bitter. She gave him her scarf. The weight of her coat and the incline of the road made her sweat. Underneath she had on a pretty black sweater with lace at the collar. The silver earrings, pressed uncomfortably inside her knit hat, were new, a Christmas gift from Drake, bought from a catalog, replicas of a Navajo design. Drake enjoyed Native American art. He longed for the deserts of New Mexico as an antidote to the Northwest winters. Cara didn't want to travel. She was happy where she was.

The road switched back. The rain fell at a hard slant. Drake lowered his head and pressed on. He wasn't slipping anymore. He went faster, outpacing her. She struggled to keep up.

The string of lights nailed to the eaves of Jackson's house swayed in the wind, giving an impression of a ship bobbing on a swell. The windows were bright. Condensation dulled the panes, making the movement of bodies within remote, even ghostly.

The living room was full of smiling people, some playing a board game set up on the coffee table. The man rolling the dice was Cara and Drake's neighbor. He nodded at them, then blew into his fist for luck. Drake went down the hall to the dining room and put his jacket and Cara's scarf on the back of a chair, occupied by Lila, the woman who ran the hardware store. She was in her seventies and known to drink like it was last call. On the table before her was an empty shot glass and a bottle of bourbon.

Cara stayed behind. She removed her hat and put it in the pocket of her coat. All the pegs in the hall by the front door were already full, so she draped the coat over the round top of the newel post at the bottom of the stairs. A toilet flushed on the floor above, and Jackson came down slowly, holding the rail as if he might fall.

"I thought maybe you weren't coming," he said.

"We ran into a ditch."

"Yeah?"

"Down the road."

Jackson nodded. He looked her in the eye.

"You've been busy," Cara said.

"Yeah. Stove finally got here. Just put her in yesterday."

It was red enamel and replaced an old black one that had leaked smoke into the room the last time Cara visited, right before Christmas. She'd brought him out some banana bread. They'd known each other casually for years. That day they'd spent almost an hour talking, she assumed because he was glad for the break in his solitude, though he hadn't seemed needy at all, just friendly. At home, Drake had asked why her sweater smelled funny. She said there'd been a bonfire on the green by the farmer's market.

Music came up. The Allman Brothers, Cara thought. She wasn't sure. But yes, she recognized them now. One had just died.

Jackson seemed inspired by the song. His body loosened.

"Nice sweater," he said.

She brought her hand to the lace along her collar bone. "Thanks."

He turned away and went into the dining room. She followed him. Drake was seated at the table, talking to Susan's husband, a round little man who prepared tax returns.

"The guy never earned a cent in his life. He inherited his father's real estate business," Drake said. Every other day he ranted about the President. Cara had stopped pointing out that Drake himself lived on the proceeds of a trust fund established by his own father years before. Not having to work was supposed to let him find a way to be useful in the world. He'd volunteered at a local food bank, then at a homeless shelter on the mainland. After that he took classes toward a degree in education so he could teach math in an elementary school, then had some sort of a run-in with one the professors, with whom Cara was certain he'd had a fling. The woman was married, the husband probably found out. Drake never re-enrolled or looked into transferring to another college to finish the degree. That had been three years before. Since then he'd tried his hand at poetry, churned out a slim volume of work that was heavily metaphorical, usually with some reference to war, destruction, or human bondage. No publisher had offered him a contract, though he'd submitted it widely. Cara ran a flower store she'd inherited from her mother, who'd died of breast cancer at the age of 44. Cara hadn't realized how lonely she'd been, how much she wanted to find a home in the heart of another, until the day Drake wandered through the door, looking for a simple bouquet for the woman he was then seeing. His pursuit of Cara was swift and merciless. He said she'd swept him off her feet.

It was he who'd done the sweeping. That passion had given way to a gentle affability mixed with minor annoyance. He made her feel old. She wasn't old.

She poured herself a glass of wine from one of the open bottles on the sideboard. The wine was fruity, which she didn't care for, so she put down the glass, took another, and sampled the next bottle in line. The vintage was better, deeper, earthier. It warmed her.

Susan was next to her, saying she should try one of the devilled eggs. Susan only came up to Cara's shoulder. She was in her sixties and wanted to be everyone's mom. She'd pressed her warmth and caring on Cara after her mother died, and Cara hadn't had it in her to accept.

Cara passed on the eggs, then plunged a carrot stick into a small dish of creamy dip. The dip was lovely, but she wasn't hungry, and tossed the uneaten part of the carrot into the deep kitchen sink. She hoped Jackson wouldn't mind. That's the kind of thing Drake complained about when she did it at home.

The talk at the table became friendlier, with laughter and smiles. Drake was the center of it.

He liked lots of people around.

She liked having only one person around.

On the screened-in back porch, Jackson sat in a rocking chair, gazing into the woods beyond the glow of his outside light. The porch wasn't heated, and he wore a heavy coat he must have kept out there for that very reason. A glass of liquor was in his hand. He turned at the sound of her approach and nodded to the empty rocker next to him.

He handed her a blanket from a neatly folded stack under the window. She wrapped it around her shoulders. He offered her a sip of his drink. She lifted her glass to show she was still working through the wine.

The muffled sounds of conversation reached them through the closed door. Cara heard Drake's voice, though she couldn't make out his words. She wondered if he had noticed her absence.

"So, you escaped," she said.

"Yeah. I'm not much of a party person."

"Me, neither."

They drank. In the dining room, a plate crashed to the floor, followed by swearing in a female voice, Lila's probably. Jackson didn't get up to see what was going on. For the moment, he'd ceded his home to the invaders.

"Any improvement?" he asked.

"Nope."

"Maybe it's time."

Cara said nothing. It was hard to think about.

Laughter came in bursts.

"Here, sit next to me!" someone said.

There followed the sound of a chair being moved across the floor. Cara hoped it didn't mar the wood. That would be a shame, though Jackson was a practical person, and wouldn't see it that way. He'd just fix it.

"A forest at night is a hell of a beautiful thing," he said.

"Yup."

"You ever wander around out there, in the dark?"

"Not for a long time."

"We could now, if it weren't so wet and cold."

"I can handle wet and cold."

He looked at her for a long moment.

"Go get your coat. Meet me outside," he said.

Cara removed the blanket. Drake was still talking to Susan's husband. Susan was a few feet away, at the CD player on the kitchen counter, inserting a new disc. The tight, twangy melody of her bluegrass followed Cara down the hall, where the board game was still going strong.

The rain had stopped. Silver clouds raced overhead, revealing, then concealing, a gibbous moon. Jackson came out the door leading from the porch, and down the set of wooden steps.

Her eyes quickly adjusted to the night. The path was smooth, and she knew he'd been working on it, removing rocks and loose branches. She didn't know where it led. He walked ahead of her and looked back over his shoulder often. The path curved, climbed, and descended next to a stream. Here, Jackson stopped. They listened to the water, the rustle of evergreen branches, and the rapid scurry of some creature in the brush.

He rubbed his bare hands together. He stopped and gathered her in his arms. His lips on hers were cold, his tongue was warm. He was so much taller than she, eight inches or more, that he sheltered her against a sudden rush of wind that caused the forest to move as one. She leaned in closer, holding him with all her strength. Her ear was pressed to his chest. She heard his heartbeat.

"Well, I suppose we should be getting back," he said.

"Yeah."

They pulled apart. They went slowly, though the cold was now penetrating. The party had amped up. Susan's joyful music flowed forth. Figures passed before the bright windows. One was alone, motionless. It was Drake, looking out into the yard. Cara stopped. Jackson did, too. They were a few feet away from the point where they'd be seen.

"Do you want to go in the back way?" he asked.

"No point in trying to sneak by. He knows I'm out here."

"Okay, if you're sure."

She took Jackson's hand, and went forward, into the light.

collector of sorrows

The little girl's tears fell like sudden rain in Nora's heart. The sorrow of a child always moved her. Their eyes were so clear that to see them clouded was agony. And there she was, in her plaid school dress, stomping her feet on the asphalt surface of the road, waiting for the yellow bus.

She was alone. No observing adult, no chattering little friend. Only that bluebird on the branch overhead. But he had his own concerns. Three crows sat silently nearby, plotting against him.

"Hi! Is it okay if I wait with you?" Nora asked.

"Who are you?"

"Nora."

The little girl nodded absent-mindedly. Her eyes were dark.

"Now tell me your name," Nora said.

"Debbie."

"That's a pretty name."

Debbie shook her head. She was in a bad way.

"Tell me why you're sad today," Nora said.

Debbie said nothing.

"It's because of your grandmother, isn't it?"

Debbie nodded solemnly.

"Because she got mad when you broke the china dog?"

"Are you friends with her?" Debbie looked more alert now, less pulled down within herself.

"I'm friends with everybody."

Debbie considered this.

"And you called the little dog 'Patches,' right?" Nora asked.

"Uh, huh."

"But, he wasn't a toy, was he? He was something your grandmother treasured, because someone she loved had given it to her a long time ago."

"I guess."

The bus would arrive soon, the driver would open the doors with a cold *whoosh*, and Debbie would climb up the steps and be gone.

"Close your eyes, open your hand, and think about Patches," Nora said.

"Why?"

"Please."

Debbie did as Nora asked. Her tear-stained face was fierce with concentration.

"Now close your hand, wait just a minute, then open it," Nora said.

When Debbie uncurled her tiny fingers, a smooth black stone lay on her smooth palm.

"Where did that come from?" she asked.

"You."

"I've never seen it before."

"No, but you've felt it, haven't you?"

The rumble of the school bus grew louder. Debbie went on staring at the stone Nora lifted gently from her hand.

Debbie wouldn't remember the incident, but Nora did. The musty patch of forest she called home was littered with many stones, each loosed from a soul in torment, carried in the pocket of Nora's green dress, and dropped quietly to the ground. Sometimes the stone bounced a further distance, some stayed right where they landed. Over time, the soil might shift, or accumulate a layer of needles from the evergreen trees all around, and the stones rearranged themselves.

This business of collecting sorrows began when Nora realized she could see inside people. She'd been called a lot of things—a psychic, an empath, sometimes even a witch. Her family abandoned her, finding her trait unnerving. No one could keep secrets around her, and people held on to secrets hard, often against their best interest.

Changing a sorrow into stone had taken time to perfect. Pain had to go somewhere, but it had to be easily carried, which eliminated the option of taking it away with her tears, or sighs, or desperate glances.

Nora had by then collected so many sorrows that the grief in her own heart was deeper than the forest night. Each stone had come to weigh on her as if it pressed into her very bones, pulling her closer and closer to the earth.

She could find another line of work. She was that clever.

You must free yourself.

She didn't know who spoke those words. Maybe no one did. Living alone could make you imagine things.

Come on. You know how.

She focused on her distress, letting it sweep through her as tears ran down and a wail escaped her lips. In her palm lay not an ordinary stone, but a flawless diamond that gave off a rainbow as it caught a sudden beam of light. This was a rare gift, and it made Nora think. It was one thing to remove pain, but what of granting pleasure?

After she left the forest, the down-and-out on city streets might find themselves holding one of her diamonds. Some kept them for their beauty alone. Many, though, sold them and found they'd left despair behind, but not always for good. Those that squandered their fortunes quickly on bad habits were soon returned to alleys and doorways. But even they hoped for better times to come again, and found that hope is its own gift, one that makes all others possible.

And as for Nora, who'd gone from stones to diamonds, she opened herself to the further mysteries of the universe until she could no longer sit, stand, or lie without pain, and then was borne away by loving hands.

good boy

Of course, he hadn't meant to. No man in his right mind would utter the name of a former lover while having sex with his wife.

Diane paused for the briefest moment after he whispered, "Nadia."

She must have heard. Why else hadn't she just kept going?

As usual, he fell asleep right afterwards, then awoke to find her side of the bed empty. That wasn't usual. He got up, put on his bathrobe, and went down the long hallway, hating the cold wood floor on his bare feet. She was in her office, a tiny warm space she'd claimed against his wishes because he'd thought his spare photography equipment should go in there, not in the garage next to the water heater, as she suggested. She was typing on her computer, bent over as she always did—she had poor posture, something she ruefully admitted. She was five feet ten, and slouching was something she'd learned as a teenager when kids at school teased her about her height. Watching her from behind, he felt a surge of affection. Diane was charming in ways she didn't recognize. She was strong, capable, and a talented chef. She dressed impeccably in brightly colored natural fibers. She loved silver jewelry. And she understood him, a little too well sometimes. When he misbehaved, even just slightly, like having one too many bottles of beer, or leaving the toilet seat up, his greater foibles could be listed out, gently of course. In that way, she was more like a mother than a wife.

"I just wanted to get this down," she said, without turning around.

How could she have heard his approach? He'd been careful to step silently.

She was writing a new cookbook. Her agent had suggested one on vegan dishes. Morris despised vegan cooking. He was passionate about cheese and meat, particularly beef. Lately he'd been presented with sautéed eggplant over garlic Na'an; rice cooked with vegetable broth and tossed with undercooked vegetables; and tofu. Lots and lots of tofu. He was certain he was developing an iron deficiency, although Diane assured him that all the dark, leafy greens appearing on his plate were chock full of iron.

"What is it?" he asked.

"An idea for carrot soup."

"Oh."

"With curry."

Curry was in everything these days. She even had tried sprinkling it over toast and blending it with sugar. He had to admit, it hadn't been too awful, but then, his taste buds were probably disintegrating on his tongue.

The thought of tongues turned his mind back to Nadia. God, that woman could kiss! They'd spent hours making out before they ever got in bed, by which point he was beyond insane. That was years ago, before he met Diane, and she didn't cross his mind all that often. Except sometimes, like tonight, when suddenly he was inside her again.

Diane closed her document, turned off the computer, and walked with him back to the bedroom, arm in arm. He enjoyed the closeness of her, and the way she could make a simple event, like going down a hall, a little grand.

She stopped at the door and looked at him closely.

"What?" he asked.

"Nothing. I was just thinking about something."

Whatever it was, she wouldn't tell him until she was ready.

*

Morris didn't like Diane's friend, Carol, probably because Carol didn't like him, although she'd never said so, and Diane hadn't, either. Physically, Carol was everything Diane wasn't. She was short, built like a fireplug, with tight, curly hair. She reminded him of a wrestler he'd gone up against in high school who got him in a half nelson five seconds in. Carol was always polite, pleasant. She asked about his work, if he were still shooting children—the play on words never failed to make her giggle—or if he'd moved on to clients who could sit still. Carol owned a bed-and-breakfast, and always had something wry to say about her guests. She was fond of gay couples, and didn't care for anyone with special dietary needs, though she realized it was her duty to try to accommodate them. Diane was a great help to her there. And when Carol came over, they went at once to the kitchen to cook and drink expensive wine. He wasn't welcome, though again, it was never specifically stated. It was the way the conversation stopped when he appeared in the doorway, or how Carol's eyebrows lifted when he asked a simple question.

He disliked Carol even more when she asked Diane to foster a rescue dog. Carol was on the board of the local animal shelter, and would foster one, herself, if she were home more. Diane said it was pretty much a done deal, unless he had real objections. Dealing with dog shit was a real objection, but she said she'd handle that. Would the dog sleep with them? No, he'd be crated in the laundry room. What if it howled all night? That was part of fostering, to teach the animal that there are boundaries, and that humans are in charge.

So, the dog moved in. His name was Buster, which Morris didn't care for. He would have preferred something more elevated, like Charles, or Phineas. Diane explained that this was the name the dog had learned to respond to. The new owners could give him a new one, of course, but until then, Buster must remain Buster.

Buster had been abused, and yet brimmed with love. He turned his moist brown eyes on Diane with a look of pure adoration. Buster was around fifty pounds, long-haired, some sort of Collie mix, and despite his good heart, was devious. He liked carrying a single shoe around the house. Then he'd drop it and wander off. They were always Diane's shoes, so she said nothing of this to Morris.

A week after Buster came to stay, Morris dreamed of Nadia. His hands were full of her raven hair. He was naked, and she wasn't, and when he woke up and analyzed the dream, he decided it represented her ultimate power over him.

They'd met on a photo shoot. She was modeling winter coats for one of the higher end department stores downtown. It was one of his first free-lance jobs, which led to others, and eventually opening his own studio where most of his clients, as Carol suggested, were squirmy, sticky children and their exhausted parents.

Nadia was Russian. Her English was poor. She communicated with her hands, and how she held her head. She laughed a lot, sometimes uncontrollably, as when he couldn't find a working power outlet, or the make-up artist dropped an entire tin of face powder, sending small billows of it everywhere. The gaiety masked deep tragedy, he soon learned. Her father and uncle had been in the war with Afghanistan. Her mother had been sent to a gulag for protesting her country's military involvements. Nadia was handed over to a vodka-swilling grandmother, who would caress her delicately one minute, and slap her silly, the next. Being beautiful in a country like Russia wasn't so special, she liked to say. Most of the women were beautiful, if they didn't get fat by the time they were 30. They only went out for a few weeks. She made no secret of not being in love with him. He made it a big secret that he was madly in love with her.

As if sensing his dreams, Buster gave Morris the stink eye, and avoided him, which suited Morris fine, even when Diane said he wasn't making any attempt to be friendly.

Then she told him he'd started talking in his sleep.

"Really? What do I say?"

"Just a bunch of mumbles."

She'd just presented him with a dish of curried tofu, and a side of white rice to which she'd added golden raisins. He was pleasantly surprised by how delicious it was. He told her he loved it.

"Thank you, darling!"

There was something forced in her gratitude. His stomach clenched, which made eating hard.

*

The weather warmed and promised another glorious summer. Business fell off a little, just as it always did. People didn't want to round up their children and beg them not to fidget when they could turn them loose on a playground, or at the beach.

Diane pounded out the cookbook all day, and long into the night. The finished draft went off to her agent one bright Tuesday morning, and two weeks later she received an offer to publish it along with a generous advance. Morris was happy for her. Diane seemed happy, too, yet there was some lurking disappointment he could hear in her more frequent sighs. He bought a bottle of pink champagne to celebrate her success and was concerned when she only had one glass of it.

"You're not . . ." he said.

"Of course not."

She always said she couldn't conceive. A pelvic infection when she was a teenager had left her permanently scarred.

"Then what's wrong?"

"Buster."

"What do you mean?"

"He seems so happy here."

She cried. She hadn't done that for years, not since her mother died. He saw how attached she'd grown to Buster, and how painful the thought of his leaving was.

"Why don't we just keep him?" he said.

Her eyes filled with watery joy.

"Do you mean it?"

"Sure."

"But you hate him."

"No, I don't."

"You don't like him, though."

"He'll grow on me."

She opened her arms, and he leaned against her, thinking how no one smelled the way she did, floral notes blended with spice, and an earthier overlay, which he glumly suspected was Buster.

The dreams of Nadia came more often, and then every night. Scenes from the life they never had were vivid, full of color and movement. They were always going somewhere. When he made love with Diane, he was silent, refusing to give himself away.

She asked him about it.

"What do you mean?"

"Well, you usually make noise. You know what I mean. At the end."

He had no idea he did that.

Then he had to assure her that he still loved having sex with her, which was true.

He wanted to ask if he still talked in his sleep and couldn't find a clever way to bring it up.

The days were long and hot. Carol and Diane sat on the shaded patio for hours every day, drinking. Carol had hired someone to manage the bed-and-breakfast for her during the whole month of July. She needed some time off, she said. She was thinking of giving it up, selling out, doing something new. They talked about opening a restaurant. That took money. Diane had inherited some from her mother. Carol was pretty flush, too. They were smart businesswomen, and could put together a good, solid plan.

Morris knew that if they succeeded, Diane would never be home. He hated the idea. He said only that he hoped it wouldn't take too much of her time.

"I've got nothing but time now," she said. He assumed she meant since finishing her book.

One afternoon, Morris came into the kitchen for a glass of ice water. His last shoot had ended just after noon. He hoped to catch up on some reading, and maybe later watch a movie. Carol and Diane were in their usual spot on the patio. Through the back door, which they'd left open, he heard Carol ask, "Is he still doing it?"

"Yeah. He can't seem to stop."

"That sucks. What are you going to do?"

"I don't know. I suppose I could talk to someone about it. I mean, there must be people who know about this sort of thing."

"He seemed like he was getting better."

"I know. That's what's so hard."

Morris stood right where he was, waiting. The women discussed a new dish Diane was going to make on the weekend, that featured both kale and swiss chard. Morris felt a weight in the pit of his stomach.

When Carol had gone home, he sat Diane down. He had something he had to get off his chest.

"What?" she asked. She was flushed from the wine. Her eyes were a little woozy.

"I just want to say I'm so sorry."

"About what?"

"Saying Nadia's name the other night when we were, you know."

Diane's brow furrowed.

"I didn't hear anything."

"You must have."

"Why?"

"Because you got up after and went into your office."

"So? I do that a lot after you fall asleep. Even on nights when we haven't, you know."

That was news to Morris.

Buster padded into the kitchen, and nuzzled Diane's hand. She stroked his head, then leaned down and said, "I'm on to you. I found it in the bathroom. I'm going to put them all up on a shelf first thing tomorrow. I've given you all the chances you'll get. Now, go and try to be a good boy."

Buster padded back the way he came.

Diane looked at Morris as if she'd forgotten he was there. Then she focused.

"Darling, who the hell is Nadia?" she asked.

He realized he'd never mentioned her. He hadn't been able to, all those years ago, even when Diane talked about the men she'd had before him. She'd even asked him if there'd been anyone special, anyone who had broken his heart, and he said nothing, because he didn't want to seem like a loser, someone still carrying a torch.

Diane went on looking at him, her head tilted, eyes growing darker.

He cleared his throat, but the words just wouldn't come.

here's why

Here's why.

You slump, shrink, curl down in your seat, never stand up straight. As if an arrow might pick you off. Not an arrow, a bullet. Not a bullet, a blow. Not a blow, words. Not words, looks.

Here's why.

You're a freak. Four inches in one year? Your father's colleague says he keeps looking for the stool you're standing on. Oh, and too bad about that limp. Too bad you're pigeon-toed.

Here's why.

You hunger to be a little girl, petite, with tiny hands, and a snappable bone. Those girls are legion. You want to absorb them, eat them up, until you become them. Only some want to become you. *I wish I could see over! Can you lift me up?* You try and fumble. The little girl has some heft to her after all. You clomp off. She finds another friend. You don't.

Here's why.

You dance with the tallest boy in the sixth grade class because he's the only one you can look up to, some sad soul in a plaid shirt who can't tell left from right.

Here's why.

Your big sister hates you, because she's only five foot four. On those three inches—the ones you have and she lacks—is written the twisted history of your relationship.

Here's why.

You cry in a closet, the closet in your father's house, the house he has with his new wife. What are you doing in the closet? Hoping to borrow something to wear. The brown and black shirt strangles you. The panty hose in the top dresser drawer only make it thigh-high. She's a tiny little thing, as your father loves to say.

Here's why.

Your self-esteem never improves. Even after physical attributes no longer rule. Even though your intellect blossoms, your talents refine, your artistic vision expands. You can't let go of having been the giraffe in the room.

Here's why.

You hate bullies. The ones who make fun of a child's teeth, or nose, or scruffy hair. You're a mother now. You show up at your daughter's school from time to time to help. You've told more than one irksome little beast to lay off, though your words are more politic. *Do unto others*, you say. You command attention because your voice is clear, your hands are gentle and dispense, brilliantly—joyously—a small delicious chocolate chip cookie as both a reward and bribe.

Here's why.

They must crane their necks so far back, and squint against the sunlight. Because you're tall.

the first time

Do you remember the first time? How the light from that candle seemed to brighten even as the rain fell harder against the pane? It was our first night away together, and the thrill of the cheat was offset by our guilt. Your wife. My husband. The lies. But love cannot be denied, even in the face of our expected loyalty and steadfastness.

Or so you told me.

After the sex—the first not in a motel, or your friend's apartment, or the back of my brother's van—we lay wrapped up like a newly formed creature, one who had never stood up straight, or held anything in its aching hands but flesh.

I had gone to see my ailing sister. You, your alcoholic uncle. My sister despised my husband and would cover any story I told. Your uncle couldn't remember the day of the week. No worries from him, either.

So how did it begin, that small spark of fury? I was talking about waking up the next day, and how maybe the rain would stop, and be replaced by sunshine and a soft, warming breeze.

Hadn't I read the forecast? Hadn't we chosen this spot on the coast because the weather was always foul? Hadn't that been the agreement, that if we went somewhere barren and remote, we could feel less rotten about our sin?

Sin?

I got up. I didn't like being naked then. I didn't want you looking at me, but it was only my eyes you saw, nothing else.

—We'll pay for this, you said. It's only a matter of time.

I was stunned. Not that we might one day regret our liaison, but that you regretted it now.

—Go, then, I said. If it troubles you so much.

You moved so fast, I was sure you meant to embrace me, reassure me, say you were sorry, oh so sorry, that you didn't want this to end, that it must never end.

I heard your blow before I felt it, so sudden and hard, like the way you make love. Even the pain was so intense there was an erotic quality to it.

You went to shower, and I sat there on the bed. What story would I tell about this bruise you'd left me with? The stumble into the doorjamb in my sister's darkened hall. Yes, I'd had one too many glasses of wine. She gave me a bag of frozen peas, and we laughed about that, remembering how our mother always demanded that we mind our Ps and Qs.

You emerged, washed clean, absolved. You'd have no story to tell, because this was all there was, this love turned to rage, then back into love as you wrapped the blanket around my bare shoulders.

I saw myself shaking free, dressing, and leaving. I would refuse your calls, and be good to my husband, whom I'd once loved almost as much as I loved you then.

But I stayed, because of the heat you bring to everything, even though it burned.

We'd never talk about it again, this first time. We might have, if it had been the last.

he said, she said

It was where movies stars used to go and rest up, be pampered, and consider the next script their agents had just sent over. A series of modest bungalows set around a beautiful turquoise pool. A waiter in a white jacket ferrying trays of drinks—cocktails, since wine wasn't so popular back then. Maybe some canapés.

Here she stopped him by holding up her hand—slim, smooth, dripping with rings, all from him, the most recent an African ruby she wore on her index finger. He joked that it was like the Pope's, given the size, the *heft*. He'd taken her hand and kissed it reverentially.

Canapés were essentially hors d'oeuvres, he explained.

She knew what they were. She also knew how to pretend she didn't know things.

Did she like the idea of staying in a place like that?

She did.

Then they'd go!

Since he'd made it big, they could do that, just take off whenever they wanted. Whenever he wanted. She was okay staying home. Their house was lovely, on the shore of a lake in western Massachusetts. Back when his books didn't sell or sold only modestly, they lived in a much smaller home where their two children had been raised. He taught high school language arts. His writing on the side, which gave him an air of burning ambition blended with the constant agony of rejection, made him a romantic character. His mystery novels were considered clever, good psychological studies of the criminal mind, the rationalization people engage in when they've done wrong.

She had worked in a bookstore part-time, then full-time after the children went off to college. When the New England winters became too much for the owner, prompting him to buy a condo in Arizona, he offered to sell it to her. The first mystery novel had just been published, and wasn't doing all that well, so she'd had to walk away. A young tech couple fleeing the rat race of Boston bought it, changed the name, invited her to stay on as their manager. She didn't have the heart.

His next book sold well and the one after that sold spectacularly well. She started writing poems again, something she'd done in high school and college, and was heavily invested in when they met decades before at the café on campus. He said she was the best-looking lady poet he'd ever seen. "Lady-poet" stuck with her.

They rented the nicest bungalow, the only one with a fireplace. It wasn't superfluous. The spring nights could still get cold there in the desert. They could sit out, gazing at the black vault of night all thrown with stars, then go inside, light the fire, and make love. He was urgent about that. Their sex life needed restoring.

His sex life had been fine without her. A pair of panties not her own came back in his suitcase. Also, a lace bra. She wondered if he stole these as tokens of his prowess, his knack of getting strange women into bed, but then she thought he'd probably just packed in a hurry the next day, leaving his hapless partner to go on her way bra-less, panty-less, or without whatever else had slid under the bed or been kicked far down in the sheets. There were unidentified numbers in the call log of his cell phone, which she checked when he was in the shower. He left it in plain view on the dresser, almost as a challenge. Then one number was named. Eileen. There were many calls from her, some text messages, too.

When will I see you again?

Not for a while.

I love you.

I told you we weren't going there.

She wanted to call Eileen's number and tell her she could have him. Then she'd see what living with a quasi-celebrity was like, though in fairness, his eye had always wandered, even before the best-seller list. His call log had been clean for the last six months. Maybe now he was trying to turn the page.

On their first day at the resort, he wanted an hour in the bungalow with his laptop. He brought his laptop with him everywhere, and tapped out a thousand words a day, twice Hemmingway's output, he often bragged.

She could lounge under the shade of a huge canvas umbrella, and scribble some of her poems. She'd resurrected a tattered notebook from somewhere in the back of her closet and thrown it in her carry-on bag at the last minute.

So he sat, and she sat, separated by no more than ten feet and a hedge that bordered the pool and lent the guest patios some privacy.

The blue of the pool was a jewel. She considered her collection. She had neither blue topaz, nor aquamarine.

Once, all she had was a thin gold band.

His face, when he slipped it on her finger.

After the money came in, she lusted. She chose the pieces, he paid for them, then referred to them all as his gifts to her. She thought it was funny that a man who made his living off words would use them inaccurately.

It was early and she was alone, watched over by palm trees, and gazing at them she dropped back to several years before, after the fourth book had been optioned for a film. Though it had never been made, the generous check gave them two glorious weeks on Maui, in a house steps from the ocean.

The palm trees in Hawaii were different from those in Southern California, but they bent just as elegantly in the breeze.

She thought about that trip, and then about this one, and how past and present are always together, how a heart *holds* them together. What did Faulkner say? *The past is never dead. It's not even past.*

With a ball point pen, she traced her hand on a blank page of her notebook. She often did this when conceiving the next poem. She supposed the habit was due to her lifelong fascination with ancient cave paintings, and the idea that someone had done the same thing, only using a stone rubbed with ash, or the tip of a burned stick. *I am here. I exist.*

The soft tapping of her husband's keyboard reached her. He was on a roll, clearly. He might be at it for hours.

On the other side of the hedge, the neighbor's patio door opened. The two lounge chairs were repositioned; something was put down on the glass table between the chairs; someone let out a long sigh.

"Leave that damn thing inside," she said.

"I might have to take an important call," he said.

"She won't be up this time of day."

"Cut it out, please?"

The breeze gusted, rippling the surface of the pool. She felt a brief chill.

A young man from the poolside bar went past with a bottle of white wine and two glasses. He didn't wear a white jacket, but a blue button-down shirt and khaki slacks. He turned and took the path past the hedge, comprised of large white stones separated by emerald green grass, to the common access point shared by all the bungalows. To reach their neighbor's patio, he would have to pass in front of their own.

He asked the couple if he could open the bottle and pour them each a glass.

"That's why we called you, for Christ's sake," he said.

"You'll have to excuse my husband. He left his manners at home," she said.

The cork came loose first with a squeak, then a soft popping sound. Liquid rushed into one glass, then the next. The glass bottle met the glass tabletop with a cheerful *clink*.

The waiter said he hoped they'd enjoy the wine, and to let him know if there were anything else he could do. He returned the way he came and took up his station at the bar where another guest was sitting on one of the stools in a pale pink cover-up, reading a newspaper. They began a conversation but were too far away to be heard clearly.

"You never let me off the hook," he said.

"Because you never change. You don't *want* to," she said.

The tapping of her husband's keyboard stopped. Maybe he was in the bathroom, or on his way out to join her by the pool. The tapping resumed.

Palm trees sway in the breeze, she wrote in her notebook.

"I told you nothing happened between us," he said.

"Maybe I should ask her about that," she said.

Hearts flatten against the gale of deceit.

How she'd wept when she knew, for certain, that he was cheating on her. She stayed because of the children. He stopped cheating, the children grew up, the cheating resumed, became more frequent, stopped again.

"You never believe me," he said.

"You never tell the truth," she said.

Why expect truth?

Truth is relative

There is my truth

Then there is your truth

It was really flowing now.

More wine was poured into the glasses. If she stood up and turned around, pretended to look for her husband, she could give them the once over. They sounded middle-aged, but perhaps weren't. Maybe the wife was fat and ugly, but probably wasn't. Maybe the man had a sinister cast, but probably didn't. They were most likely ordinary people, caught up in an ordinary struggle, where pain had become a relative thing.

Absolutes blur

Edges turn soft

Like the line of my jaw

She didn't mind the idea of aging. He told her once she would be a beautiful old woman. And he? He had always been too handsome for his own good. That would never change.

Another gust of wind nudged her umbrella. The woman at the bar laughed and put one hand on the brim of her wide straw hat. A cocktail glass was on the counter at her elbow.

"It's too cold out here," he said.

"I suppose you want to go in," she said.

They stood up, each huffing a bit with the effort. Their patio door closed. Angry muffled voices leaked out from inside their bungalow. Her husband must be hearing them, assuming he wasn't completely absorbed in his work, which he probably was.

She used to wonder how much she could take. Though it never got easier, she discovered she could take a great deal.

Her husband's cell phone rang. He answered it.

"I asked you not to call me," he said. Their own patio door closed. She couldn't hear his voice then. The fighting couple had quieted, too.

The wafered trunk is a miracle of strength

Graceful, resolute

She put down her pen and closed her notebook. She descended the three shallow stairs into the warm blue water. She swam to the middle of the pool and went onto her back. The sky overhead was clear; the mountains were rocky and jagged. The water filled her ears, and whatever few sounds had been audible were silenced. She closed her eyes and drifted, feeling only the water on her skin, finding the words she'd add to the page when she got out:

It can bear any cruelty, any blow, any offense, any slight

You once could, too

But no more

moonlight on the bay

As the rain got heavier, people moved inside. When the annual Art Walk was held in good weather, everyone stayed out and enjoyed the spring twilight. Last year's mild temperature and clear skies meant poor sales. Tonight, just about every place was packed. Moving among the paintings on display was difficult, and some business owners grieved the occasional drops of water shed by hastily closed umbrellas, even as they celebrated the occasional keen interest in one or two pieces.

Celia was soaked. She'd had to walk into town because her boyfriend, Terry, had been working swing shift all week at the hospital and just didn't have the energy to get off the couch and give her a lift. Might she borrow the truck? Just for tonight? He reminded her that it was less than a mile, and that she was always saying how she needed to get more exercise. Celia was a cashier in an upscale grocery store and found that hours scanning jars of imported olive oil, Oregon bleu cheese, and Japanese eggplant didn't do much against the thirty extra pounds she carried, even though she was on her feet the whole time. When she reminded him that it was raining, he gave her a tired look that just said, "don't." He told her to take his jacket, which was waterproof. On his days off he hunted or went fishing, depending on the season. He was a man who knew how to brave the elements.

The jacket was miles too big. The cold penetrated easily. Her track shoes squished with each step, and her feet were going numb.

But the art lured her on. She was a sometimes painter. Her fortieth birthday had been a big wake-up call. If she were going to make something of herself as an artist, she needed to work a lot harder. Terry was sympathetic. He said turning 40 had been a kick in the balls for him, too. He was a custodian and didn't know how much longer he could go on emptying bins of medical waste just for a lousy paycheck. Celia knew that if he won the lottery, he'd quit his job in a New York minute. Then she'd never see him. He'd be off somewhere with one of his weird friends who tended to either be in rock and roll bands, or work for the sanitation department, or both.

And if she could get up in the morning and do what she wanted? Well, paint, of course. But also spend more time seeing her mother who suffered from multiple sclerosis and was confined to a Medicaid nursing home at the age of 61. Then there were her sister's three boys whose company she enjoyed a lot, except when they were hungry, or fighting with each other, or most recently when Trevor, the youngest at seven, threw up his chocolate milkshake all over the back seat of her car. That was months before, and it still smelled when she sold it, after deciding that walking everywhere was good for her health.

A group of young people stood outside the door of a popular diner, laughing and smoking. One girl had green hair. A man had large gauges in his earlobes. Celia tugged involuntarily at her right one as she passed. She'd always found that look hideous. Some people wanted to make themselves ugly as some sort of statement, which was what, exactly? That beauty was bullshit?

She made her way toward Marla's, a lovely gift shop that also had a good selection of work by local artists. Someday Celia's watercolors would show there, with higher and higher price tags as time went on. Clarion was a small town in the South Sound Region of Washington State and just up the road, was Seattle. That's where the money was, art-wise. The galleries there were the goal, financially speaking. But money and art were poor bedfellows, weren't they? How could you put a price tag on what came out of your soul? Then again, you had to pay the bills. Commerce and creation had to get along, somehow.

She was momentarily distracted by a set of four drinking glasses that were nicely etched in broad, wavy strokes. She'd taken a glass blowing class once and adored it. Her vases were always lopsided, and the instructor eventually despaired.

Next to the glasses was a set of hand-embroidered napkins that struck Celia as fussy, and too old-fashioned. And on the shelf below them was an assortment of small leather-bound journals. She picked up the one with a lavender cover, and turned the blank pages, thinking she could use it to sketch in. The twenty-five-dollar price sticker on the back dissuaded her.

Toward the back of the room several people were gathered next to an old man in a wheelchair. All of them were considering a watercolor in a heavy wood frame Celia saw at once was all wrong for the delicate shimmer of the image it contained. *Moonlight on The Bay* was full of blue and black tones, balanced against yellow and green. She approached and inspected every inch of the picture, led by the subtle changes in hue from one patch to the next. She was smitten.

The man in the wheelchair was the artist. He was telling the people around him that he had decided not to sell the watercolor after all, because it needed a little something more. One woman protested, and said it was perfection itself. He waved her off with a bent, gnarled hand.

"I absolutely agree. It's amazing," Celia said.

The old man looked up at her with tired blue eyes.

"Only the artist can say if a work is finished or not," he said. He asked Celia to take the picture off the stand and hand it to him. She lifted it, held it about eighteen inches from her face, and gazed at it longingly. Then she set in his lap.

She asked his name. He gave her a card from the breast pocket of his blazer that said Charles Lawton. Just below was a telephone number with an out-of-state area code.

"Like the actor, only spelled differently," she said.

"How can you possibly know about Charles Laughton? You're too young."

"I'm an old movie buff. In that I like old movies, not that *I'm* old, but you just said that."

She sounded like an idiot, but Mr. Lawton didn't indicate that he thought so. The group had moved off. He asked if she would mind pushing his chair towards the door. His driver would be bringing the car around in a minute.

She got behind the chair, waited for him to release the brake, and nudged him forward. She went very slowly, not only to avoid crashing into an expensive display of bone china, but because she wanted to talk him out of not selling the painting. Then it occurred to her that she probably couldn't afford it, anyway.

"I take it you're an artist, yourself," Mr. Lawton said.

"Yes."

"Media?"

"Watercolor, as luck would have it."

"Watercolor hasn't been particularly lucky for me. I do better with oils and pastels, but I keep getting called back."

"It's the only way I can truly express myself."

The rain hadn't let up. Mr. Lawton's driver wasn't there, so Celia parked him to one side of the entrance and helped herself to a hand-painted rocking chair. After a moment it occurred to her that the salesclerk giving her the eye might not appreciate her butt gracing a piece of expensive merchandise. She didn't care. She had Mr. Lawton all to herself. Even better, he let her look at the watercolor up close again.

How had he managed that blue in the middle of the bay? Had he blended cobalt and lavender? That's what she would have done, and suggested this, but he was distracted by the arrival of his driver, who turned out to be his grandson in a pickup truck that had seen better days.

The grandson was deft. He got Mr. Lawton into the passenger seat quickly, then returned, folded up the chair, and put it in the bed of the truck under a thick tarp. Celia waved good-bye as the truck pulled away. Neither man saw her fond gesture.

She had the next day off. She set up her easel on the porch, barely warmed by a low-voltage heater she borrowed from the bedroom. The furnace was dying, and they were trying to do without it. The landlord had not yet responded to their messages about its pending fate. Celia suggested they just replace it themselves. Terry said she obviously had no idea how much a furnace cost, which was true.

She pulled out her last work-in-progress, a marsh. The cattails were well proportioned, and their hue was right, but the grasses were too blue. She added some yellow to lend a greener shade. It worked. She preferred realism in art, though admitted that some painters, who pushed the boundaries of color, like Picasso and Van Gogh, were geniuses.

The sky was a subtle mix of gray, purple, tinged with red. Dawn or dusk? Dusk would have murkier tones, she thought. Dawn would sparkle. Or was that too predictable? Couldn't dawn rise drearily, and dusk fall brilliantly?

Stop tripping yourself up and concentrate!

It was hard to. She was pulled back to *Moonlight on The Bay.*

The rain let up the following day, and her walk to work was complicated by huge puddles along the shoulder of the road. Terry had complained about what she'd made for dinner the evening before. She'd overcooked the rice, because she'd been trying to work and get a meal on the table at the same time. Terry used to cook a lot when they first got together. He was pretty good at it, too. His specialty was spaghetti with browned garlic. He hadn't made it for her in a long time.

At 11:30, she ate her lunch as she always did in the employee break room, which was sparse and dreary, at odds with the elegance of the rest of the store. The overhead lights hurt her eyes, and she made quick work of her chicken sandwich. Her supervisor, Drew, came to say that someone was out front looking for her.

It was Mr. Lawton's grandson, who removed his baseball cap as she approached, then shook her hand. His palm was rough.

Mr. Lawton was doing poorly and wondered if she could come by and talk about the painting some more.

Celia asked if he had decided to sell it after all. The grandson—Luke—wasn't sure; he hadn't said anything about selling it. He just wanted to talk to her about it.

Celia asked how Luke had found her. He'd gone back to the gallery and asked someone there. The lady he'd talked to knew Celia well, and where she worked, and so, here he was.

"That would have been Maureen. Tall? In her sixties?" Celia asked.

Luke looked vague. He clearly hadn't taken note of her appearance.

He wrote down their address on a paper napkin he got from the hot soup kiosk. Celia said she didn't get off work until four. She added that she had no way to get out there, so could he come back and pick her up?

Luke thought about it. He said he'd try.

The hours slowed to an impossible crawl. Her distraction was noticed by more than one customer, and by Drew, who said it was hard to be efficient when one's mind was elsewhere. Drew was a gentle boss. Celia loved her dearly.

Four o'clock came, four o'clock went. Celia waited twenty-five minutes in the cold, then walked towards home. Luke pulled up beside her.

"Sorry. Battery died. Had to get a jump," he said. She climbed into the truck. On the dashboard was a bobblehead of SpongeBob SquarePants. The cab smelled of cigarette smoke, but the ashtray was clean.

They made their way towards Hays Harbor, a remote, wooded section of Clarion. It occurred to Celia that she could be headed to her doom. Luke was spindly. She could probably fight him off. She remembered that she hadn't told Terry she was going to be late. Her phone wouldn't get a signal out here, in any case.

A light rain fell. The wipers were bad, and the windshield was soon streaked and hard to see through. They turned onto a dirt road through thicker woods, at the end of which stood a large, handsome home, brightly lit and inviting.

Luke told her to go on in, the front door would be open. He needed to get the truck into the garage. The door was heavy, with leaded glass at the top. It led to a generous, open space with a kitchen on one side and a huge stone fireplace on the other. The walls were covered with paintings, decorative plates, African masks, and stunning black and white photographs. What hung there was better than anything in the downtown Clarion galleries. If she ever won the lottery, this was the kind of house she'd have.

Mr. Lawton rolled his chair up a side hall and stopped. He stared at Celia, then held out his hand. She walked over to him and took it in hers.

"Here you are," Mr. Lawton said. He told her his studio was the first door on the right. She pushed him back the way he'd come and turned the corner into a room with a high ceiling and skylights. There were several easels set up, each with a work-in-progress, including *Moonlight on The Bay*, which he'd taken out of its frame. Next to a ceramic mug full of brushes were tins of paint. Some hadn't been touched in a while. Others glistened with recent use.

"There," Mr. Lawton said, pointing to the lower portion of the painting where the moonlight shimmered. Celia bent down to look. The yellow shade contrasted harshly with the water's blue. It hadn't looked that way in the gallery. He'd been working on trying to make it right.

"More white? A hint of gray?" Celia said.

Mr. Lawton nodded. He lifted a brush from the mug with a trembling hand.

"You," he said.

"Oh, no, I couldn't."

He pushed the brush at her. She took it. Her face was warm, but her fingers were cold. She dipped the brush in the glass of water on the side table, then put the tip into the tin of white paint, then into the one containing gray paint, and with excellent precision applied the bristles to the paper. She stood back. Mr. Lawton leaned forward. The moonlight had taken on a soft silvery tone that worked perfectly with the deep blue of the water.

He told her it was just fine.

"Thank you."

"Now, sign your name below mine."

"I can't do that."

"You must."

"But, it's *your* painting."

"Not entirely. Not anymore."

"Mr. Lawton—"

He pointed with effort.

Celia painted her first name. The letters were too large, she saw, and made Mr. Lawton's signature seem small and insignificant.

He told her the painting was now hers. She was not to refuse. It could not go to someone who didn't know it as she knew it, who had not completed it, as she just had.

Luke came into the studio and asked Mr. Lawton if he wanted some tea. Mr. Lawton winced at some sudden pain, then shook his head. He told Luke to drive Celia home.

"I'm sorry I can't ask you to stay longer. I'm rather tired at the moment," Mr. Lawton said.

She removed the painting from the easel and shook Mr. Lawton's hand. His eyes were damp.

On the way back to town, this time in Mr. Lawton's much newer sedan, Luke said Mr. Lawton wouldn't finish the other pieces now. He was all used up.

Celia cradled the rolled paper in her lap.

But I'm not.

yellow

More trees in the mountains went up, and the firelight was yellower than the day before. He called it the color of dry sand. The sun reddened, as if not in anger, but in grief. Who wouldn't mourn? Homes lost, people evacuated, men exhausted from no way to quench the flames. Blackened skeletons were left behind, not just trunks and branches, foundations and chimneys, but bodies, too. They didn't talk about the bodies on the news. Too graphic. A burned-out house was one thing, its fallen roof horrible to imagine, the crash and whoosh as it dropped, but consider the man or woman alone, probably old, maybe asleep, or too sick to get out of bed and flee. How often did that happen, though? Who knew? They used to burn people alive in olden times, always heretics, and sometimes just because the king was particularly pissed off at some traitor or other, and felt a swift end by the blade was too kind. And the fossilized remains from the eruption at Pompeii in 79 AD showed many had been asleep at the time the river of burning lava met their flesh. He'd seen a house on fire once. Flames made a sound, like wind, and the heat could be felt from far away. The smoke rose thick and black, twirling at times, as if some dreadful joy were felt.

She said watching the news upset him and he should stop. Then she said dwelling on things he couldn't control should also be stopped. But no one controls his thoughts, does he? Can't be done, unless you're drugged to the gills on something so strong your brain is like a smooth amber lozenge, frozen, lifeless.

He thought of water instead. A case of opposites. Water conquered fire, but it also killed. It raced down canyons, swept away houses, cars, boats, trailers, sheds, fencing, families, their pets, furniture, everything they'd ever touched in their whole lives. It pounded coastlines, rolled over villages after an earthquake at sea, making people scramble and climb, climb, climb, not all escaping, so many swallowed by the smacking, muddy mouth of an angry ocean.

Water roiled with earth and debris had a yellowish tint, didn't it? Didn't she see the connection?

She reminded him that they were in a land-locked state. A tsunami was impossible. And could he please change the channel?

She'd had to get rid of every yellow thing in the house. The tablecloth, napkins, throw pillows, their bedspread, towels, even the plates. It was her favorite color. A cheerful color, she would say. A happy color. He might have agreed once, but since the last tour, when two of his men burned up in a Humvee, he couldn't have the faintest hint of it near.

It hadn't gone so far as demanding that she remove the daffodils from the garden, only because he didn't go into the garden. He didn't go outside. He hadn't set foot over the threshold in four and a half months.

"You're like that man in *To Kill A Mockingbird,*" she said. "Boo Radley."

He'd never heard of it.

"A voluntary shut-in."

Maybe they could have people over? Different faces might be nice? Then he wouldn't have to leave the house. He told her to forget it. When she was invited to the neighbor's barbeque, she went alone. Everyone understood. His affliction wasn't unique. The street was full of veterans. She wore a yellow dress. Her clothes were spared the purge because she flat out refused. Unlike the other items she'd tossed out they were personal, chosen with care.

She asked him to help her with the zipper. He didn't come near her. She knew he wouldn't. She could see his face in the mirror she stood before. What was in his eyes then? Had fear, for an instant, been replaced by rage?

Anger is a healthy emotion, the neighbor said. He was a therapist. He'd urged her husband to get help. He didn't get help. She sipped the gin and tonic he gave her. When it went right to her head, she sat in a lawn chair shaded by a stately cottonwood. Those trees defined the West to her. Coming across the Colorado Plateau that first time, you knew where the shallow rivers were from the clusters lining the banks.

There were other hard yellows besides flames and dirty water. Bruises were yellow, too. He didn't hit her. But he gripped her arms, held her in place, as if she were the only thing keeping him on his feet. She had to wear long sleeves, even when it was warm. The dress she wore now was sleeveless, and her arms bore the traces of his most recent clutch. Eyes were drawn there, as she continued to sit, loving the gin in her blood. Then a kind hand was on her shoulder, so warm it almost smoldered.

He could have gotten them out before they burned. He said so a million times. But he froze, and wasn't that funny? How can one freeze in the face of an inferno? The truth was, he was scared. Terrified. In every dream since then he'd rushed in and emerged unscathed.

"So, get yourself out now," she told him. "Before we both burn up."

The neighbors talked about the smoky air. Maybe they shouldn't be adding to it, with their hamburgers and hotdogs.

"Life goes on," she said.

She was offered another drink and accepted it.

What if she sat there, until he came for her? He wouldn't come, night would fall, the smoke would clear, the stars would twinkle in cold merriment.

Tomorrow all yellow things could turn green, or red, or blue. She might burn her dress in the kitchen sink and set off the smoke alarm. With yellow gone from the world, did he have a chance? Did they?

Someone brought her a paper plate of food. It was meatless, out of respect for her vegetarianism. She put her drink on the grass and sank her teeth into the buttery ear of corn. Then she consumed the macaroni salad. Someone mentioned grilled peaches would be for dessert.

She put down the empty plate and looked across the street.

"I'm going to paint the house this summer," she said. Polite faces turned her way.

"What color?" someone asked.

"Like a newborn chick. Or a Meyer lemon."

Someone chuckled.

"That'll make a statement," someone else said.

Later, she'd remove all the pictures from the walls, most of which were from their wedding and early anniversaries, patch the holes, and do every room in the same damn shade.

people like them

He landed a good gig. Looking in on people's homes would keep them in Aspen. The hikers were gone; the skiers yet to descend. Those in town now were there for the golden trees, and the occasional red and orange ones the dry summer had miraculously produced.

The management company had turned him down at first, though his record was clear. It was because he was Hispanic, he thought. But so were the road crews, the waiters, the bellhops, the maids, and the servers in the Mediterranean restaurant.

He'd grown up outside of Boulder and saw the town change into a high-tech mecca. His parents had sold their home and fled to Arizona, where another branch of the family was installed south of Phoenix. But Raoul couldn't go; wouldn't go. Those Rockies held him fast, and he held them just as fast in his yearning, hungry heart.

And for what did he hunger and yearn? Everything, starting with those stone mansions, occupied for maybe one or two weeks a year by millionaires who lived in New York, Dallas, Seattle, Denver, and one family from Honolulu who must have thought snow was an exotic delight.

He hungered also for Sally, who'd gotten up her nerve and moved up there with him, though to be fair, all she'd left behind was a job she didn't like processing Social Security applications, a mother she didn't speak to, and an ex-boyfriend who tried, every other month, to get back on her good side.

Raoul was 31; Sally, 35. Her blonde hair and blue eyes enchanted him.

Opposites attract, she said, though they weren't opposite really, but very much aligned. Sally hungered, too, not for money, though God knew it helped, but for some spiritual space she could occupy and just be.

His job was to visit seven homes once a week; make sure that all the lights worked, the faucets ran; the grounds were lovingly mown, trimmed, and raked, though if he had to guess, the guys who came out in their tan shirts didn't really give a shit; and the interior dusted and mopped per whatever schedule had been arranged. Then, when an owner was on the way in, make sure the refrigerator and pantry were stocked according to pre-selected specifications, which usually included a lot of high-end champagne, French cheese, and Belgian chocolates, subject to change at the last minute, of course.

The arrangement was particularly convenient because the homes were within walking distance of their apartment, paid for by the management company, in the fancier part of town. High-end location aside, it had six hundred square feet and no mountain view. The windows rattled when the wind blew, and the wind blew all the time.

Sally got a part-time job in the bookstore, because they happened to be hiring the day she wandered in looking for a guide to local hiking trails. She didn't know anything about books. The manager said she'd learn. The off-season was always quiet, and she'd have time to get up to speed on new titles, mostly memoirs and mysteries, before December, when the skiers lit up the town. Christmas in Aspen was wild.

The weather went from crisp to freezing overnight. This meant Raoul had to assess the heating system in each home. Since they'd all been built within the last two to three years, the furnaces were in good shape. Still, he got a service guy out to make sure, Lloyd from Leadville. Raoul saw nothing funny in that alliteration, but Lloyd sure did. His mother, after being unwilling to relocate to the middle of nowhere so her husband could work at the Climax Mine, underwent a change of heart and assigned each of her five children a name beginning with L. Lola moved to LA; Lester and Larry were still local; and Lisa, also local, was expecting her first. When asked how her angel would be christened, she said Mary, not for religious reasons, but because M was the next letter in the alphabet.

The Parson home had two furnaces, and each needed a new filter. Strictly routine. Only Lloyd didn't have any and would have to order them special. He got in his truck and waved to Raoul as he backed down the steep, curving driveway. Raoul stood a moment in the garage to watch him go. He pressed the button to lower the door, made his way across four parking bays, three of which were occupied by a Porsche, a BMW, and a Mercedes SUV, to the door that led into the kitchen.

This was his favorite property. It had over eight thousand square feet; two master suites, both on the main level but on opposite sides of the house; floor to ceiling windows that gave on the slopes and the forests beyond; a jacuzzi surrounded by twining vines in a wrought-iron trellis; and a kitchen with two islands, two dishwashers, a six-burner Viking range; and three wall ovens. The art he didn't really understand. All of it was modern, abstract, emphasizing color over subject. The floors were a rich honey color, decorated with heavy Persian rugs. Leather furniture was everywhere, and very comfortable to sit on, though he knew he wasn't supposed to.

There was top-notch liquor on a wheeled cart in the den, a spacious room with wood beams in the ceiling and a stone fireplace. He helped himself to a crystal tumbler and a generous pour of bourbon. There was wood and kindling ready to go, but to light a fire would be insane. If someone came to the door, he could ditch the drink and say he was just closing up, but smoke from the chimney would tell a very different story.

The surrounding homes were empty. He knew because they were on his list. Their outside lights came on automatically at dusk, which it was just then becoming.

He called Sally and told her to get over there.

"Where?" she asked. She had just finished her daily yoga routine and was sweaty head to toe.

He gave her the address.

"Why?" she asked.

"Time to party."

"Huh?"

He explained.

"You'll get in trouble," she said, though she liked the idea a lot.

"No one around for miles. Who's to know?"

She showered and dressed in her usual jeans and pullover sweater. She seldom bought new clothes. She didn't like thinking about appearances, hers, or anyone else's, though of course she noticed what everyone wore, and whether or not he or she (usually he) were attractive. It was part of her inner dilemma, one she'd always had, between desire and acceptance.

Raoul was waiting for her in the driveway, wearing a smart leather jacket she'd never seen. He ushered her into the empty bay. Next to the Mercedes Sally's twenty-year-old Corolla looked pathetic. She pinched his sleeve.

"Nice," she said.

"Guy's got four more. You should see the closet."

"Are you sure this is okay?"

"Yeah, why not?"

She explained that most home security systems had a feature that let the owner see when doors were opened and closed. If someone really wanted to study the activity, the long time spent in the house would be hard to explain.

Raoul looked down at her skeptically. Her ex-boyfriend had worked for a home security system in Boulder, which is how she no doubt came by this knowledge.

"I'll say the cleaning crew didn't show, and I took care of it myself," Raoul said.

"Well, they don't know you, so they might believe it."

Raoul didn't clean anything, something on which Sally occasionally remarked. He thought she was too fussy about things like that. He said if she didn't do it, he would, eventually. To her this meant when the place became intolerable.

He showed her the house. In one of the master bedrooms there was a vanity table with bottles of perfume. Sally brought a couple of them to her nose, found one she liked, and dabbed some on her wrists and behind each earlobe. Raoul stared. He was surprised. She explained that in high school she'd worked in a department store selling cosmetics. Maybe that's where her disdain of fashion and finery came from, he thought.

The shower stall was enormous, with two shower heads. They stood in it together, fully clothed, and thought about what it would be like to use it every day. Sally said you'd never want to leave. Then there was the soaking tub, big enough for three people. That made her laugh. What kind of relationship put three people in a bathtub?

He asked if she'd brought the sandwiches he'd told her to pick up at the store.

"Yes."

"What kind?"

"Roast beef for you, like you said."

"What did you get?"

"Ham and cheese."

They were in the kitchen at that point, sitting in a pair of plush upholstered stools, their elbows on the island, a slab of white marble that had gray and blue veins running through it.

Raoul said they couldn't eat food like that in so nice a kitchen. Sally asked what else he had in mind.

The refrigerator was empty. The freezer contained fancy microwavable meals. Nothing appealed. He told her to go get the sandwiches from her car. She came back to find that he'd opened a bottle of French wine and poured some into two crystal glasses. She didn't know he could move that fast. But then, Raoul was full of surprises. The wine was stored in a climate-controlled room behind the kitchen. He'd scoped it out on an earlier visit.

"They're going to notice," Sally said, and tasted hers. It was smooth and rich. All the wine she'd ever had in her life was nothing compared to this.

"You worry too much."

"Maybe you don't worry enough."

They ate quickly and in silence. They realized they'd have to take their trash out with them.

"We should get out of here," she said.

"Not yet."

They wandered the house some more. In the room where Raoul had found the bourbon was a wall of bookshelves and an attached ladder on wheels that you could slide left or right and then climb. Sally went up it and chose a book, a history of the Roman Empire. She flipped through the pages. The lettering was small and hard to read. She put it back and chose another, this time one on the botany of South America. She put that one back, too. The next book she picked was a novel, written in the 1930s about a woman named Harriet Lowe. She pulled a pencil out of her back pocket which she'd taken from the store after filling out the order for the sandwiches, crossed out the name on the page, and wrote in her own. Then she crossed out her last name, so no one would track her down.

The whole time, Raoul had stood below, drinking his wine, gazing out the window into the purple evening. Stars were out. The trees were black. She joined him. Their reflections in the glass made them seem insubstantial, almost ghostly, and when he put his arm around her waist, it was as if a phantom had brushed her.

What if this were their house? Would the image before them become more solid? She felt cold, standing there, so she turned away.

Back in the kitchen, she poured herself more wine. Some spilled on the counter. She pressed the sleeve of her sweater onto the droplets, but a pink stain remained. She wet her finger and pressed hard, rubbing back and forth. Raoul asked what she was doing. She told him. He looked and said there was nothing there.

"Are you sure?" she asked.

"See for yourself."

He was right. The surface was clear.

She put her face in her hands for a moment.

"Are you okay?" he asked.

"I don't know."

"Too much wine."

"Only had a little."

He put his glass down next to hers, took her in his arms, and kissed her sweetly at first, then with more intensity. She'd said before that she liked being kissed that way. She was slow to respond, then did, forcefully.

He led her into the other master bedroom. It had a four-poster bed with a thick, embroidered cover. Against the wall was a charming writing desk that held several beautiful glass paperweights, full of swirling colors. She wanted to touch them, bring one to her cheek and feel its coolness, but he didn't let go of her hand.

They lay on the bed, kissed for a while, stopped, and were still, side by side.

"You know, we've got a perfectly good bed at home," she said.

"Squeaks."

"Yeah."

She laughed. They'd wondered before what the people next to them must think.

She closed her eyes. She could be anywhere, even in her childhood room in the small home shaded by a tall cottonwood tree in Greeley. As an only child, her private fantasy life was rich. She lived in many different houses, all splendid, quiet, gracious, nothing like the one where her parents fought nightly, and her mother shared her bed when she couldn't stand being close to her father.

She opened her eyes and registered the luxury around her. She didn't want to live where people had so much more than she did. Better to be where the field was more level. She could tell him she wanted to go back to Boulder, but there was too much money there, too. Other people would always have more, and people like her and Raoul just had to accept that. There was no point thinking anything else. If he didn't see that now, he would have to, before long.

"We should go," she said.

They got up, smoothed the cover and pulled it tight. They removed all traces of themselves. He put the leather jacket back in the closet and put on his denim one he'd dropped on the carpeted floor. He turned out the lights in the rooms they'd been in, and for a moment, they stood in darkness looking out into another darkness. They cast no reflection then, yet she felt firm and steady on her feet.

On the short drive back to their place, they agreed a house like that wasn't all that great, really.

"Didn't feel very cozy, did it?" he asked.

"Not at all. It actually felt sort of lonely."

"Yeah."

"Might sound funny, but I like our place better."

"Me, too."

She put her hand gently on his leg while he drove. The winter was going to be all right. She could feel it.

i know you

It's slow, even for a Tuesday. The rain slicks sidewalks, streets, doorways, every corner of Olympia. The homeless find shelter where they can; under bridges, in the parking lot behind the abandoned industrial park, protected by flimsy tarps, donated tents, anything that isn't soaked or flooded. People scurry past the picture window, heads down, hands in pockets. No one carries an umbrella. Northwesterners can't be bothered.

At the end of the bar George Thomas sits solidly on his favorite stool, watching the ballgame on the screen mounted to the wall. The volume on the television is off. The players stand poised, then move suddenly in response to the pitch, soundlessly, as if in a dream. At a four-top near the door the Banners hunch over their frothy mugs. They're newlyweds, regulars, uneasy in each other's company. Serenity asks if they need anything else, and the wife, Lisa, looks at her with pain in her eyes as her husband says they're fine.

The Banners are a stellar example of why people shouldn't marry. Once that ring goes on, it becomes a chain, Fidel says, which is why he and Serenity have lived together for twenty-six months with a clear understanding that no knot will be tied. He watches the game; Serenity polishes glasses that she's removed from the dishwasher. The hard water leaves spots. She's added that special liquid that's designed to take care of them and never does. She's told Fidel about it several times. He tells her the glassware is her department.

He's a good bartender. He hasn't been stumped by an order in a long time. The book he keeps under the counter was his father's, who worked in one of the big hotels up in Seattle before he shot himself in the head. Fidel doesn't talk about it, but Serenity knows Fidel's mother made the man miserable. She wanted things he couldn't give her, and in time, his sense of guilt led him to pull the trigger.

Serenity's tired. She works too hard. She cooks, cleans, manages their money, when they have any. They're usually broke. The rent on the bar takes a huge chunk. Business has been bad for months. Last year, when her mother died, Fidel closed the place for two days. He said it was the right thing to do, but the lost revenue added to her grief.

The Banners go on their way. George Thomas has another beer. The baseball game continues. At the bottom of the seventh, three young women come through the door, shrieking, laughing, running their hands through their soaking hair. They're dressed up, high heels, stockings, lots of jewelry. Maybe they're students, but Serenity doesn't think so. Students at the local college shun fashion, feminine trappings, no glitz and glam for them. Maybe they're down from Seattle, though there's much more to do up there.

They take a table. Fidel is out from behind the bar before Serenity can get there. He offers to hang up their coats. The blonde on the right gives hers to him without a word; the brunette says the back of the chair is fine for her; the blonde on the left hands over her leather jacket with a smile the size of the Ritz.

Serenity thinks of her own hair, which is half blonde, half black. The dye job is working its way down, her God-given raven shade replacing what came from a bottle. Fidel doesn't like her with light hair. She doesn't look like herself, he says. Because Fidel is handsome, he wants other people to be attractive, too. It bothers him when they're not, especially women. He won't have any trouble with the three at the table. It's clear they know they're good-looking. It's almost as if they're competing for who will win the pageant.

Left Blondie's a shoo-in. Her sweater is tight, her breasts ample, her neck long and slim. The crucifix dangling from a thin gold chain only adds to the allure. Fidel is a lapsed Catholic and used to tell tales of what Catholic girls are really like.

He takes their drink order, and scurries back to the bar. He's amped, almost nervous, and splashes soda water down the front of his denim shirt. Serenity goes over to the table, and asks the girls for ID. They stare at her. She asks again. Wallets are exhumed, licenses slid out and handed over. Right Blondie is Cheryl, age 22. Brunette is Megan, age 24, and Left Blondie is Julie, age 23. Serenity reads Julie's last name.

"I know you," she says. Julie stares at her sullenly, the brilliant smile gone.

"I don't think so."

"Your family lives on Division."

"Who are you?"

"Nobody you'd know. But I knew your older sister, Lacey."

Julie holds out her hand for her license. Serenity returns it, and the others, too.

Fidel appears, drinks on a tray, which he deposits with a flourish. The women laugh. Serenity doesn't. Back at the bar, she says that's Lacey Sandhurst's baby sister over there.

"Who?"

"You remember. You worked on her car."

"Oh, yeah. '67 Mustang. Lived down the road. Saw me tinkering with my Chevy. Asked if I could help." He wipes down the bar, leans into it hard.

"Uh, huh."

"You never met her, did you?"

"I thought I ought to, you talked about her so much."

"Just about the car."

Lacey showed up at her door one night when Fidel was out with a friend, looking at a truck he wanted to buy. She played it cool and asked if she could come in because her power was out and she needed to make a call. The square shape in the front pocket of her blue jeans looked a lot like a cell phone to Serenity. She let her in anyway. Lacey asked if Fidel were home. Serenity said no, he'd be back in a while. Lacey said to tell him she needed to talk to him, and he knew what it was about. Serenity said she'd be sure he got the message.

She never told him about the visit. They'd be watching TV, and his cell would buzz in his pocket. He'd look at the screen and go into the other room to take the call. He'd say it was his friend with another truck he might look at or wanting to borrow some tools. Once he said it was the bank calling back about the loan he'd applied for. It was after eight in the evening. Serenity said that banker was dedicated as hell. Not long after, the Mustang and Lacey were gone. The phone calls stopped. The loan fell through, he said, but Serenity had set up online access to their accounts. The loan came in and went to Lacey. Five thousand dollars. Just like that.

Serenity figures it was to get rid of a baby, not to have and raise it. Kids cost a lot more than five grand. She hopes she was wrong, because she doesn't like the idea. People have a right to be born, don't they? And to be happy? The Declaration of Independence even says so. And as for the liberty it also guarantees, boy, does Fidel take *that* one to heart.

Now here's Julie, who looks so much like Lacey it's driving Fidel nuts. Serenity bets he recognized her the minute she came through the door. Did she pick their bar because she knew Fidel worked there? That seems like a stretch. But Fidel is a man women go out of their way for.

Her mother warned her. "He's got a roving eye," she'd say. After she got sick, the comments were harsher. "All charm and no personality." Her mother never got to know him, not the way Serenity knew him. And what she knows is that he loves her, truly, but can't stay true.

Women leave men like that for less. Women stay with them if there are children or money on the table, neither of which Serenity has.

George Thomas says it's time to pack it in. He pays his tab, and meanders across the room in a slight zigzag. He stops by the table where the women sit. He bids them a lovely evening and makes for the door.

"God's sure crying tonight," he calls back over his shoulder. No one answers. He leaves.

At the bar, Fidel tells Serenity he has an idea. Something to boost revenue, bring people in, even on bad nights like this.

"Ladies Night," he says. "You know, half-priced drinks for women."

"It's sexist."

"So? If they come, the guys will, too."

"Call it something else."

"Like what?"

"Ovary ovation."

"Get out."

"Unsung uteruses."

"What's wrong with you? I think it's a great idea."

"I don't suppose that table had anything to do with it?"

"What, them? No. I've been thinking about it for a while."

The three women order another round. Half an hour later, they want a third. They're visibly tipsy. Julie has her eye on Fidel. She's flushed. The ball game concludes. Looks like the Astros won. Fidel tells Serenity the ladies are too drunk to drive, and he's going to call them a cab.

When he goes to the table to make his offer, they all groan, protest, giggle, and flirt. Julie says maybe he's right, but she's got her car a block over. She hands him the key. They all live near each other. He can drop her off last. One of her brothers can drive him home. Fidel confirms where she lives, and says he can walk, it's only about a quarter mile. She says it's raining. He says he doesn't mind getting wet.

"You look like the cat who got the cream," Serenity says when Fidel fills her in.

"Can you close up on your own?"

"I've done it before."

He leans in for a quick kiss. She gives him her cheek.

"I won't be late," he says.

"Bet you will."

"Why do you say that?"

"I know you."

He doesn't hear. He gets his jacket on, runs Julie's credit card for the tab, hands it back, and helps them into their coats. They walk out and head up the sidewalk, four across, arm in arm. Serenity stands at the door, watching them go. She turns the sign on the door from Open to Closed, and flips the latch. Before she lowers the blinds on the window she looks up at the sky, where the rain has stopped, the clouds have moved on, and a riot of stars are thrown in an ordered chaos, like wishes that will never come true.

silent auction

Liane had to get rid of the statue. She was downsizing. A widow of two years, with no more children underfoot, didn't need a four-bedroom home. The condo she put earnest money on was charming, but small, and the statue would take up too much room.

Frank's aunt had carved it as an art student in Germany before the Second World War. A woman, a Jewish woman, studying sculpture always struck Lianne as bold, almost wild, but Frank's description of his mother, who survived Auschwitz, differed. Maybe the war changed her into a quiet soul, given to long bouts of melancholy.

Her younger sister escaped the Nazis with some family belongings, among them the statue. It was three and a half feet tall, and heavy, so her efforts were particularly heroic. The aunt, Frieda, always felt her older sister's talents worthy of respect. She put a chain with the Star of David around its neck—its abstract neck, which was just a round projection near the top—and prayed for her sister's safe return.

Rachel, Frank's mother, made her way to the Chicago area after recuperating in Sweden. When the Americans rescued her, she weighed eighty pounds; a walking skeleton. She met Frank's father at a bakery in Skokie. They had three children. Frank's siblings were long dead, one from cancer, the other from a car accident. Frank and Liane found different nooks for the statue once they bought their home. Sometimes it was in the living room or bedroom, then in Frank's den where he could look at it when he tired of grading papers. He taught high school math. Most of his students didn't care about the complex relationships among numbers. Some did.

Liane had taught English at the same school, until she retired last year. The school held an annual fundraiser for extras the district didn't provide for, like music, art instruction, or a senior trip to the nation's capital. Some people thought the money raised should be used to buy sports equipment for the football team, but they were overruled every time.

Liane planned to bring the statue to the fundraiser, and let it go to the highest bidder. It was a silent auction, held during a dinner that cost twenty dollars per person and featured one chicken dish, and one beef dish. There had been a heated discussion about introducing a vegetarian option, so this year a pasta primavera would also be available.

Liane was a sturdy woman and worked out with free weights three times a week yet getting the statue to her car was difficult. She thought of calling her son, who lived nearby, but he was at work and would not appreciate the interruption. Her daughter lived out-of-state and had for years. She hadn't gotten along with her father very well as a teenager, and the rift sadly became permanent.

When Liane reached the school, she asked the janitor to lug the statue in for her. He obliged, not altogether nicely, since he was in the middle of eating his lunch. Liane gave him a ticket to the fundraiser, saying he should come and enjoy the food, and not feel pressured to bid on anything unless he wanted to. He slipped the ticket into the pocket of his olive-green shirt.

The fundraiser was two days away, yet the reorganization of the gym was in full swing. Items for sale were lined up against one wall. There were the usual home-made atrocities like kitchen oven mitts; placemats; lopsided ceramic vases; bookmarks; a basket of stuffed animals; some old hardcover books dating from the 1940s and 1950s; and a lovely hand-painted scarf. Liane's statue was the most interesting thing there, and looking at it, her heart contracted.

She was pulled back all the time. She had assumed there'd be a gradual acceptance of absence. Instead, she pined, yearned, longed, and hungered. Here is where her flair for language, which always annoyed her composition students, now felt like an added burden. Frank's death had been sudden, which though merciful for him, was cruel for her. She'd had no time to prepare herself. They were looking forward to retirement, making plans, thinking of relocating out of the frigid Midwest to the Arizona sun where Frank could take up golf and Liane could turn her artistic talents in a new direction, painting perhaps, or resume pursuits she'd let go for one reason or another, like weaving and an intense love of needlework.

He went to the store, stood in line, and dropped dead. A vessel in his brain gave way. At the funeral she stood with scores of colleagues and her son. Her daughter sent her flowers but didn't attend.

Jill approached her briskly. Liane dreaded speaking with her. Jill was too much of everything—kind, sympathetic, caring. Being around her was like wiping spilled honey from your blouse. But Jill gave her the quickest hug, said she was looking just great, and that she'd see her at the dinner, where they could catch up. They were close friends, once. They'd been in the same department. Jill would retire at the end of the year. Liane was glad she'd be living across town in the new condo when Jill had all that free time on her hands.

On the little card that would sit next to the statue Lianne wrote, *A fine example of pre-Holocaust sculpture.* That would either invite bids or turn people away. For a moment, she regretted selling it. But she had to. It evoked too many memories.

She arrived early for the fundraiser and walked around the decorated gym. Round tables with six folding chairs each were covered with dingy linen tablecloths. Cool jazz flowed from the speakers mounted on the wall. One half of the floor was occupied by rectangular tables displaying what was for sale. On the second one, someone had put a Cuckoo clock in front of the statue. There was room for both to sit side by side, so Liane put the statue next to the clock. She repositioned the bid sheet, too.

There was already an entry on the bid sheet. $700.00. The 7 had a line through the stem. This was a common way to write the number in Europe; France in particular. Liane knew only one person who wrote sevens that way. He wasn't French, but he'd lived there as a child.

She forced herself to breathe deeply and slowly. She even closed her eyes, realizing that if anyone were watching her, her behavior might cause alarm.

She opened her eyes. There was no one there.

She hadn't heard he was back. But then, why would she have? They hadn't been in touch for years. Had he recently learned of her loss, and returned? Why hadn't he tracked her down, if that were the case?

She sat at one of the round tables where she could see the door. The dinner wouldn't start for over an hour, so she might have a long wait. She kept looking at her phone, though it was pointless to. She had a different number now.

This is stupid!

Someone else might have made the bid. She wasn't going to wait around for a man who walked out of her life years before.

He stood in the doorway, gazing around the gym. He was very much the same. More gray in the hair, a bit rounder in the stomach. In a moment he would see her. She'd stayed too long.

She approached him from the side. He turned just as she reached him. The smile he gave was warm, the wordless embrace warmer still. Though in his arms only for a few seconds, she wondered how she had managed to live without them.

"Liane."

"David."

He seemed shorter, and she realized she was wearing heels. She slipped them off. He looked at her feet and laughed.

"What are you doing?" he asked.

"Reclaiming a necessary proportion."

He kissed her cheek. She asked if he'd come all the way from New York for the fundraiser.

"I moved back last year," he said.

"Missed the Midwest weather?"

"No."

He was sorry he hadn't looked her up before. He didn't know if he should.

"How did you find out about the auction?" she asked.

"Oh, quite by chance. I wandered over here just the other day, sort for old time's sake."

He'd taught Math with Frank for years. Then he got a job in the east, at a small college. It was quite a career advancement, after teaching high school.

"You knew I'd retired?" she asked.

"I did the math. No pun intended."

He was surprised to see the statue. In fact, he couldn't believe it, because he'd been thinking about her so much, lately. And here it was.

"And you bid on it," she said.

"Couldn't pass it up."

"It's not worth seven hundred dollars."

"It's worth more."

She blushed.

The week she had the house to herself because Frank was at a conference, and her son was visiting her parents downstate, washed through her. The statue had stood in the bedroom then. They always mentioned it, afterwards. David loved its smooth organic shape and asked if Liane's mother-in-law had had Lesbian tendencies. The affair continued after Liane learned she was pregnant with Stacey. They stole every moment they could. David's wife worked the night shift at the hospital, and Liane told Frank she was at Jill's, grading papers because it was quieter there. Jill agreed to cover for her. Jill didn't like Frank much. David divorced his wife when Stacey was two. He begged Liane to leave Frank. He said Stacey was still young enough. He wanted her to grow up with her biological father. Her conception came at a time when Liane and Frank weren't sleeping together as often, which convinced both her and David of her parentage. For all Frank's accuracy with numbers, he never paid attention to her cycle, and met the news of her second pregnancy with joy. Liane was moved by David's plea, but couldn't tear her family apart. She told herself she was noble, doing the right thing, but the truth was that she was terrified.

Had Frank sensed that Stacey wasn't his? She wondered so often if that's why he was so cool with her. As she grew, Stacey was cool in return. Their distance made her regret her decision to stay, until one day she understood that she and David would never have been happy. David wasn't a calm person, Frank was. David raged at her when she said she wouldn't leave her marriage. In truth, he was so upset, she thought he might hit her.

"If you really want it, I'll give it to you for free," Liane said.

"I couldn't ask you to do that."

"I don't mind."

"Why are you selling it?"

She explained. He, too, recently bought a condominium, but nowhere near hers. If she ever wanted to see the statue, it would be an easy enough drive.

He didn't used to be coy. She remembered him as direct, blunt. "I want you more than I ever wanted any woman."

He never used the word *love*. She did, often. It had astonished her to discover that she could not only love two men at the same time but be *in* love with both of them.

She said he could take the statue with him now, if he wanted. He went to the table and had no trouble carrying it out. She put her shoes back on and removed the bid sheet and card. She followed him, aware that she was still flushed.

His car was new. He put the statue in the trunk.

"Liane," he said.

"David—"

"I came back because of you."

"Frank died two years ago," she said.

"I thought I should wait until you retired."

What wasn't he telling her? She could guess. A relationship had ended, and now he was at sea, needing companionship, moral support, a woman's touch. Since he left his wife there had no doubt been many relationships. He was searching when he found her; he was searching still.

She wasn't.

He closed the trunk of the car.

"How is Stacey?" he asked.

"Both the kids are fine."

He nodded.

"Well, I should let you go," he said.

"Yes."

He hugged her again. She held onto him hard. Then she stepped away.

"Say, give me your number," he said. He took out his cell phone from the pocket of his coat.

She hesitated. She could make one up, but that seemed ridiculous. She gave it to him. He tapped the numbers into his contacts list. Maybe he'd never call. Maybe he'd call the moment he got home.

"We really need to catch up," he said.

"Of course."

She drove off, along a route she knew so well the twists and turns would stay in her mind forever, framing a way to tell him they already had.

a wild feeling

Losing love is like the season's thinning light. You know it's coming, yet it always takes you by surprise. Summer marches down through the mountains and onto the beach just the way a man descends on your heart. He's happy there for a while. You find a rhythm. Then the wind blows from a different direction and the sun slides lower in the sky.

With the town so full of people, the emptying is hard to imagine. Its arrival brings regret. Wanting the sidewalk all to yourself, then wishing you weren't walking on it alone. Getting through the line at the store in a jiff, then wishing you'd had a little more time to stand and overhear little bits of other people's conversation, other people's lives.

The exodus never fails. Labor Day is the last big crush of bodies everywhere.

Sadie's business falls off then, too. She sells salmon burgers over the counter of a food truck. What she had to go through to get the city council to let her do it still irks. Crystal Beach isn't that kind of town, she was told. They want to keep their tony atmosphere. Yet it's the owner of one of higher-end galleries that comes to her defense, citing freedom of expression, of all things. He takes her to dinner afterwards at La Reine. Over the coquilles he tells her he admires a woman who's practical, business-minded. When the second bottle of Château Lafite Rothschild has been opened, brought from the climate-controlled wine cellar and held by the waiter as adoringly as if it were the baby Jesus, he asks her if she'd like to have an affair.

She does.

Why not?

An exchange of physical pleasure isn't the only thing on offer. He wants to back her financially.

She doesn't understand. She owns the truck outright.

What if she were to expand her business? Have more than one truck? Maybe, one day, a whole fleet?

"Why would you do that?" she asks.

"I'm in love with you."

It's not the first time she's been told this. It's taken years, but she finally accepts that she's beautiful, even at her age.

Derek's 49. She's 51. He's divorced; she's never been married. Neither has children. He wants to take care of her because he's lonely, though he doesn't say this. He's bored with his own success. He wants to be excited for hers.

They sleep together a couple of times. That is, they try to. He can't manage it. Each time, he apologizes. She sees how hard it is for him to accept the loss of his virility. Can't he take something for it? He would, for her. If she became his. She can't do that, and he says he really didn't mean it. They remain friends. Nothing more is ever said of his financial largesse. Or of love.

That was over a year ago. Winter comes and goes. March brings the day-trippers out from Portland, and some loose-enders up from California—people who work seasonally, pitch tents beyond the town limits, and can't afford the expensive restaurants. Which makes Sadie's truck a big draw. Artists, many of them. A few photographers. One woman develops a sudden hard crush, and begs Sadie to pose nude, in candlelight. Sadie does.

Why not?

The shots are taken at Sadie's place, a two-bedroom cottage back in the trees where you can hear the ocean but not see it. The woman, Laura, thinks it's charming. She asks if she can move in, take the second bedroom.

"In exchange for what?" Sadie asks. Laura looks miserably at her hands, thrown carelessly in her lap.

"I'll clean and cook."

"Are you a good cook?"

"No."

"Maybe I'll teach you."

Sadie says when it no longer suits her, she'll ask Laura to leave, unless Laura goes on her way, first. The look in Laura's eyes says she doesn't think that's likely. Laura's 31 and obviously looking for a mother—a mother for whom she lusts, but Sadie doesn't draw hard lines around love. Love tends to break all rules and customs.

As the spring rains drive people indoors, business is spotty at the truck. Sadie doesn't mind. She's frugal; her savings account flush despite the low season. She sits in the back and works on her needlework. She has a passion for needlework, developed in childhood at the knee of a grandmother whose hands always held thread, yarn, silk, floss, anything she could make something beautiful and vibrant out of.

The current canvas is an abstraction of muted color. It would be a shame to make it into another decorative cushion to sell at the crafts fair in Portland. She doesn't do the selling herself, that's handled by Marie, a weaver and painter. She goes up every summer when the fair runs weekends along the Willamette. Sadie's work is always admired, less often bought. But still, it brings in a few dollars. Marie taught Sadie how to weave, and a small loom sits in her cottage, unused. Sadie thinks she'll change that, this year in fact. She's been stuck, she realizes. Too comfortable. Too predictable.

Easter comes, and Sadie treats Marie, Laura, and Derek to a leg of lamb. Her mother taught her the recipe years before. Sadie thinks often of her mother, and the unhappiness she endured at the hands of her father. She thinks of her sister, too, who always took the father's side. What little the man had went to Sadie's sister when he died. The sister lives on the east coast. She and Sadie don't talk. There's nothing to say, because there's no love between them.

After Marie and Derek leave, Laura does the dishes and breaks down crying. Sadie tries to get to the bottom of it and can't. In the morning Laura tells her she's leaving, going home to Indiana where her brother offered her a job as a bookkeeper in his auto shop. She's never going to make anything of herself as a photographer, she sees that now. Sadie says dreams take hard work. Laura asks Sadie what her dreams are, what she works for.

At the moment, Sadie can't think of anything to say.

Her mood suffers, as a result. Laura's departure makes the cottage feel larger than it really is. Sadie's not used to loneliness. She's not used to feeling unmoored. Her dreams are full of waves rising over the bows of ships, of sliding into freezing, murky depths.

The third week of April is stormy. Rain falls daily, sometimes hard, lashing the beach. Business is terrible. Sadie closes up the truck and stays home. She even calls Derek to see if he wants to come over for a spirited game of Scrabble, but he doesn't answer. She remembers him saying over dinner that he was going to Europe. She could have gone with him. He'd have been glad to take her.

She drops by Marie's. Marie lives in a leaning two-story house on a bluff, left to her by a grandfather who'd developed sections of the Oregon Coast. His estate had been cash-poor, which means Marie is now, too, something she always says is freeing in its way. She knows what limits there are on her life, which lets other limits, like on her creativity, disappear.

She's not alone. Her nephew's out from Iowa, thinking about relocating over the summer. The nephew is Nolan, an old family name, Marie explains, as he and Sadie shake hands. Nolan says Marie talks about her all the time, which Sadie's sure isn't true. Nolan's one to curry favor, that's clear. Sadie doesn't mind. She doesn't mind at all.

He needs work. Sadie might take him on. Can he cook? Operate a grill? Is he good with the public?

Marie says he can charm the skin off a snake.

His blush throws Sadie into a panic, the kind that only a handsome man can cause.

She knows it's going to happen yet doesn't rejoice. It's always hard to lose her heart to someone.

He likes that she's older. He says it gets certain problems out of the way.

"Like what?" she asks. They're at her place, the sun rising through the trees. She sits at her vanity, brushing her hair. She's let it grow to her waist. She thinks now of cutting it. Nolan lies in the rumpled sheets, smoking a cigarette, though she hates the smell. Every time he lights one, she thinks to mention it, and every time she doesn't.

"Insecurity. Lack of experience," Nolan says.

"You find women your age insecure and inexperienced?"

He thinks. "They all just want babies."

Nolan is 34.

Sadie had wanted a child at that age, too. The man she was with didn't. She considered going it alone, then thought it would have been unfair to the person she brought into the world.

Nolan pats the empty space in the bed next to him. Sadie regards him in her mirror. Her eye traces the curve of his bicep. She wonders if her teeth left a mark.

What makes him different from all the others? Not his intelligence, which is slightly above average. Not his sexual skill, though it's pretty damn good. The color of his eyes? The shape of his mouth?

Just the way he makes her feel. As if, when he's inside her, everything makes sense.

Is she simply living out the cliché that he completes her, and makes her whole? No, she's already complete and whole. What he does is make the world whole.

She wonders what he'd say if she said so. She hasn't decided yet if he's cruel. It doesn't matter, really. She can handle cruel.

She holds out her hand to him, and he gets up and comes to her. He stands behind her, then bends down and kisses her cheek. It's a devoted, worshipping kind of kiss. As a girl, she'd once kissed the marble foot of the Virgin that way.

He's a good worker at the truck. Fast, accurate, cheerful. He takes over making the coleslaw, and she admits it's better than hers. In the evenings they walk on the beach. The town fills up, and the beach is crowded. Still, they go. He's drawn to the waves. He stands and watches them for a long time. Sadie wishes she could be so easily awed. But this is what time does to us, isn't it? Takes a bit of the wonder out of things.

He doesn't lose any of his shine, though. If anything, he glows under her attention.

Her connection to him deepens until she wants him to disappear inside her, stay a while, then come back out with something of hers imprinted on him. Something he'll never lose.

Maybe she's being vain, or possessive, or just nuts, she's not sure. This desire to absorb a man hasn't happened to her before. It's a wild feeling, and she loves it.

An old girlfriend hits town, someone he'd left behind in Iowa a couple of years ago. Dana. Her head's shaved. She wears a thick leather band around her neck and on each wrist. Her face is chiseled, not gaunt exactly, just very well-defined. She's not beautiful, but she's interesting to look at.

As to brains, it's hard to say. When she hangs around the truck, she barely speaks. But Nolan always seems to know what's on her mind. He doesn't say how long they were together, but it's clear that duration wasn't as important as intensity.

Sadie feels him change. He quiets, pulls into himself, touches her with less heat.

When she finds herself crying in the shower, she takes herself to task. This is the way it is. When he says he's moving out, she says nothing. He's kind about it. He doesn't want her to feel like he's gotten tired of her.

"What, then?" she asks.

He doesn't know.

Nolan quits the food truck so he can get ready to leave Crystal Beach. He and Dana haven't decided yet where they'll go. California, probably. Dana comes by to pick up his last check. Sadie gives it to her through the service window. Dana looks at her. What's in her eyes? Regret? An apology? Does *she* want to absorb him? Return him in an altered state?

Sadie thinks it's okay, in the scheme of things, to impute her mad urges to another woman.

"Give him back," Sadie says.

"No."

"You don't understand."

"*You* don't understand."

It doesn't matter. She might not be up to it, anyway.

Sadie buys wool in shades of red for the unused loom. She sits in her cottage and works that rigid heddle like a pro. Nolan comes by. He says he's broken it off with Dana, that he's been a fool, that he can't leave Sadie.

"Yes, you can," she says.

He sits beside her and cries.

He tells her his affairs have always been scant, in terms of the heart. Even with Dana, he says then. Sadie's the *one*.

How can she say that here's the proof that she changed him? Given him something he didn't have before?

She holds him. He stops crying. She tells him how it is with her. She has nothing more to give him. He needs a woman who has love stored up.

He asks where love goes. She doesn't know. She's never known. Out there somewhere, with the waves and the sand. Maybe that's what the gulls sing about every day, as they glide aloft. She tells him to go and find it.

When he leaves town, Dana stays behind. Sadie offers her Nolan's old job at the truck. Dana asks why Sadie would hire her. Sadie says she needs help, and has no hard feelings toward her. Dana accepts. She's adrift and angry. She speaks bitterly about Nolan.

"If you're so upset, go after him. He shouldn't be hard to find," Sadie says.

Nolan's in Eureka, California. He texts Dana his address and tells her to drop in whenever she wants.

"Why would I do that? He'd just up and leave again," Dana says. She's exchanged her leather bands for silver beads. Sadie finds it an improvement. Her hair's growing out, too. It's the lightest blonde Sadie has ever seen.

"Probably," Sadie says.

Dana looked accusingly at Sadie.

"What?" Sadie asks.

"You drove him away."

"It was over."

"He didn't think so."

"He did when he told me he was leaving town with you."

Dana concedes the point.

Sadie tells her to watch the salmon on the grill. It's smoking. Dana flips the filet expertly. She catches on fast.

The lunch crowd thins, then dies off. Business is slower each day. Sadie tells Dana she won't be able to keep her on through the winter. Dana says that's cool. She'll figure something out.

The sorrow in her eyes brims. Sadie's heart is heavy, too. Another's misery is never easy to bear. Dana lifts her eyes. They soften when they see Sadie looking at her. She kisses her on the mouth. Sadie doesn't pull away. She's never been with a woman, and is pretty sure it won't be as good, but maybe the world, now whole, can be further enhanced.

As Dana reaches for her, Sadie thinks, why not?

the shed

The shed sat behind the house, deep in the yard, shaded by Western red cedars and big-leaf maples. A bank of sword ferns grew along one side. Wildflowers, grown from seeds thrown by a former owner, softened the other side. Behind it was a tangle of branches and small logs that gave into the deeper forest of their property. The wood shingle roof was a surprise. You wouldn't think someone would spend that kind of money on a shed. Money had also been spent to install two large windows, one in front and the other in back. Really, to look at it, you thought more of a child's playhouse than a place to store rakes and hoes, bags of potting soil, hoses, and a pair of woman's gardening gloves the previous owners had left behind. The gloves were small. They didn't fit Marjorie at all. She held them with a twinge of dismay, because she'd never liked her big hands, though they'd been very useful to her for over sixty-five years. Her husband, Ed, had big hands, too. He'd been an accountant, and year after year his sturdy fingers served him well, pushing his pencil over the pages of endless ledgers and legal pads. Though he was good at it, he didn't like it much. He never complained. Unhappiness seldom came out of his mouth.

Now, in late summer, with the garden blooms drooping towards the ground and the light just beginning to thin, Ed rehabilitated the shed. He moved everything it held outside and bought three-quarter inch plywood to replace the flimsy floor. He had a good table saw in the garage and went to work cutting the pieces to fit. Marjorie left him alone. Retirement was hard for him. For decades he hadn't had enough hours in the day. Now, there were too many. Marjorie wished he'd spend more time with her. With their children living out-of-state, and many of her friends enjoying vacation homes in sunnier places, she felt isolated. But, to be fair, she'd often felt that way over the years. She told herself she should be used to it. When it bothered her too much, she started another quilt. She was proud of her quilts. She sewed every one by hand. She copied vintage patterns, made them fresh with bright colors. Her studio was a rainbow of fabric scraps. She worked in a comfortable chair before three south-facing windows. She'd fallen in love with the room when they first toured the home two years before and claimed it for herself.

From where she sat, the shed was clearly visible, as was Ed, going back and forth between it and the garage. He wore the khaki slacks that were the staple of his work wardrobe for years. The button-down shirts were replaced with heavy flannel ones. He looked like a man who would have been happy living in the woods his whole life. Marjorie supposed she might have taken to that kind of life herself in an earlier day, if they'd have been settlers, for instance, carving up the forest and selling their lumber. She might have taught in a one-room schoolhouse, instead of the ugly beige brick building where she tried to shape young minds for forty years. Even then, with thirty fifth-graders in the same room, she'd felt alone.

She pinned a row of red and green triangles together. She was making a Christmas quilt for her daughter whose first baby was due around Halloween. The quilt was intended for the crib, but Marjorie knew Elaine wouldn't want it there. She'd prefer something simpler, less *precious* would be the word she'd use. It was important for Elaine to reject Marjorie's overtures. It was her way of punishing her for not taking right away to Connor, the man she dated in college and then married. Marjorie had nothing against Connor, except that he was boring. She tried to express this delicately to Elaine, who picked up on her meaning fast enough.

"So's Dad," she'd said. Ed wasn't boring. He was just quiet. Connor talked a lot and never said anything startling or unusual. Elaine was spirited and full of life. Why had she chosen such a dullard?

"Because he's reliable. Solid as a rock, really," Ed had said. Connor was a dentist. Marjorie couldn't imagine anything worse than peering into people's mouths all day, but she kept that to herself. Elaine and Connor lived in Portland. They came up every month. Marjorie never invited them; Elaine always suggested it first. She'd quit her job in retail when she got pregnant, and was restless, Marjorie thought. She grieved for how Elaine might feel after the baby was born, stuck at home, exhausted. Connor's blandness might drive her mad, then. She hoped it wouldn't.

Their son, Raymond, was a musician. He lived in Baton Rouge where his wife's family was from. Elaine and Connor went to see Raymond at least once a year, something that might change with the baby around. Raymond sometimes came at Christmas. Marjorie and Ed hadn't been down to see him since he moved away. She wanted to go, Ed always said they would, then nothing was done about it. She supposed Ed had travelled enough on business to last a lifetime. She didn't feel that way, herself. Her close friend Susan and her husband had just bought a home in Arizona, and from there went all kinds of places. Marjorie wanted that kind of life, too. The idea of going anywhere alone didn't appeal. But then, with Ed so quiet and lost in his own thoughts, what would the difference really be?

At the end of the week, when the first rainy day closed down upon them, Ed said he was going to lay an actual floor in the shed.

"Why?" Marjorie asked.

"Nicer."

"What kind of floor?"

"Something easy, durable, you know."

He went to the hardware store and returned with several boxes of laminate tile. Years before he'd attempted some home improvement in the leaning Victorian they owned. At the time, he wanted to remodel the downstairs bathroom, and got as far as pulling out the old plaster and lath. The bathroom sat with bare studs for months, until Marjorie convinced him to hire a contractor.

Elaine called and said they couldn't come up that month because her doctor had put her on bed rest. Marjorie asked if everything were okay with the baby. Elaine said he was fine.

"He?" Marjorie asked.

"It's a boy. We did genetic testing because I'm over 35. I told you that."

"I guess you did. But not what gender the baby was."

"I just found out."

"Are you happy?"

"About it being a boy? Yes!"

Elaine said her blood pressure was iffy, and the bed rest just a precaution. She wanted to know how she and Ed were, if he were still messing around with that stupid shed.

"He's turning it into a palace," Marjorie said.

"Good lord."

"It's good for him to have a hobby."

"I suppose."

Elaine had to go; she was feeling tired. They hung up.

By the time Marjorie had stitched together over half of her new quilt, Ed had laid the floor in the shed. He wanted a rug to go over it. Marjorie didn't understand. He said he was going to convert it into a sort of study for himself.

"What? Why? How will you heat the damn thing?" she asked.

He didn't know. Maybe he'd just bundle up.

"What are you going to do for light?"

"What they used to do in the old days, kerosene lanterns."

"Use one of those low-energy LED lanterns, instead. Kerosene smokes, and that's no good in a small space." Ed conceded the point.

Marjorie was baffled. They bought this big house for him to have his own study, a place to read and think. Why on earth would he prefer that stupid shed?

Because he was making it over the way he liked. Marjorie had chosen the furniture for his den soon after they moved in. She always asked what he wanted, what he wasn't crazy about, and he always said her choices were fine. She saw now that he hadn't cared at all what she put in there, despite her working hard to find the right color rug.

It was that fake-Persian rug he wanted to put in the shed.

"Really?" Marjorie held her coffee mug in mid-air. Ed was still behind the newspaper; the vantage point he'd made his announcement from.

"You chose it for me, correct? And it's mine to do with as I like?" he asked.

"Oh, go on and take it, if it's so important."

An antique writing desk soon joined the rug out in the shed. Then a leather chair that adjusted in several ways—up, down, tilting forward or back, with a separate lever to support the lumbar with more or less pressure. Marjorie asked him what he was going to do with a desk and chair.

"Write, what do you think?

"Write what?"

"My memoirs."

"Very funny."

He put his arm around her shoulder and said he was sorry for being such a bear. He was going to try his hand at poetry. Did she think that was awfully silly of him?

"No, not at all, if that's what you want."

The rain fell. Ed went to the shed each morning and came back to eat lunch and charge his laptop. He said he wasn't getting much done, and wished it were going easier. She suggested he give up the laptop and write with a notebook and pencil.

"I'd think the best poems would always want to start with a pencil," she said.

He went out to the local bookstore and came back with a small notebook with unlined paper. He said the idea of writing on lines felt too confining. She agreed. Sometimes in the classroom she encouraged the kids to write a story on construction paper so their words could rise and fall of their own accord.

Ed applied himself, but with poor results. He decided he was no poet. Marjorie said he should write a story about something important from his life, when his understanding of something changed. She could see him think of Raymond wanting to become a musician. They'd fought about it off and on most of Raymond's teenage years. Marjorie pushed for peace, begged for understanding, and failed. Raymond pursued his dream. Ed grieved that he hadn't been as brave when he was the same age, or as lucky, or as free of the desire to be financially secure. Marjorie had met Ed when he was twenty years old. He knew what he wanted out of life. Then he got it. Now he was disappointed.

The weather worsened, and rain fell for days. Ed put on long underwear beneath his slacks and a thick sweater under his insulated jacket. He brought books out to the shed and read them. He took notes on what they made him think about. He walked around the trees, writing down what kind there were and how many he saw. He came inside for lunch and again for dinner. Every evening Marjorie hoped in the morning he'd stay, and every morning back out he went.

Marjorie finished the quilt. Elaine called to say she was fine, that they were getting excited for the baby.

"Just now?" Marjorie asked.

"You know what I mean."

Marjorie didn't. "Of course," she said.

Raymond called. He said he heard Dad was building some kind of fancy shed. Marjorie filled him in.

"Maybe he's channeling his inner tough guy," Raymond said.

"He's just looking for something."

"You'd think he'd have found it by now."

"You wait until you get old."

"You guys aren't old."

Marjorie was glad he called, but then she wanted to get off the line. She asked him to stay in touch. She knew he probably wouldn't.

One day, Ed stayed out longer than usual. Marjorie could see the light from the battery-powered lantern glow in the early dark. He didn't come in for dinner. She wrapped herself up in the quilt she'd just made, put on her rubber boots, and went out to the shed. She knocked on the door. A moment later he opened it and stared at her.

"I'm not standing out here in the rain, if that's what you got in mind," she said.

He told her to come in. The only place to sit was in the chair he just vacated. He offered it to her. She shook her head, and sat on the floor. He lowered himself back into the chair. It was cold enough to see her breath. She asked why he didn't come in for dinner. He said he'd been thinking.

"About what?" she asked.

"Dying."

"There something you're not telling me?"

"No."

"Well, think about something else."

He asked how she liked the shed. She looked around. She said she liked it fine, though it was colder than hell.

He nodded. He asked if she'd like a drink.

"Of what?" she asked.

He pulled out a flask from his pocket. He said no, he hadn't been out here drinking if that's what she was worried about. She said she wasn't worried. He offered her the flask. She removed the lid and drank. It was a good single-malt scotch. She handed him the flask, and he drank, too. Her knees and hips began to ache, there on the floor. When she mentioned it, he took off his thick jacket and told her to sit on that. She did. It helped.

He said he felt like life was one long road. She nodded. He said it had been a pretty smooth one, just the usual bumps and sharp turns.

"You mean Raymond," she said.

"Yes."

"And Sarah Beth."

"Not that again."

Sarah Beth was a woman in his office who had a crush on him. Marjorie admired his candor in telling her, then thought it was his way of explaining that he liked her, too. Maybe they slept together, maybe they didn't, but the suspicion lodged in her mind. Passing time has covered it with all the things that happened since then. Sometimes the cover frayed, and the idea was fresh and hard to bear.

He said he hoped she was still happy with him.

"Sure."

He passed her the flask. She took a long drink.

She looked at him. He was still handsome, still unassuming, only there was something different in his eyes. Not fear exactly. Just a keener light.

"Is that what you're doing out here? Figuring I got sick of having you around?" she asked.

"No."

"Or did you get sick of having me around?"

"No!"

"Well, then what you are doing out here in this freezing dump?"

He laughed. Maybe he was just seeing how much he could bear, he said. She told him to take up a better hobby. He laughed again.

"So, what do you see up ahead? On this road, I mean," she said.

"Not sure yet."

"Well, when you figure it out, let me know."

"I will."

The rain fell harder. Marjorie's toes were going numb.

He took another drink. She did, too. The wind rose, and branches scratched the back wall of the shed. To Marjorie it sounded like something wanting to get in. Not menacing, just persistent.

She held out her hand so he could haul her to her feet. She rose with a grunt and looked down at him.

"Okay?" she asked.

"Okay."

He stood up and picked up the lantern. They went across the yard, not bothering to hurry out of the rain. Later, she stood at the window and looked out. She couldn't make out the shed at all in the dark. Not even the white trim around the windows showed. It was as if it had melted away into the forest. But it would be there in morning, solid and cold as ever. Maybe Ed could get a small wood stove for it. That would be a great project. When she suggested it, he agreed, only he was done with the shed for now, and would think about it later when the weather improved, maybe in the spring.

first cut

It wasn't the first time she wanted to take one home. They always stood so nicely behind the chair discussing the basics, her history, likes and dislikes. Then when the ice broke, they dove in, lifting it by the handful, saying how rich and thick it was, and such a lovely silver. And they all said it matched her blue eyes, though one used the term *brought out*. Her hair brought out her eyes. All that attention warmed her heart.

And believe me, this was a heart in need of warming.

It's not a hard-luck story, let's be clear. Sid did okay in life, financially speaking. God knows it didn't hurt to be the only child of a cold ruthless social climber whose only interest was making money.

Eddy the Plume, she called him. He wrote the most awful novels—bodice-rippers, manly men with swords in hand, cheesy characters worming their way into innocent, hungry hearts. And Eddy knew all about that. Boy, howdy! Sid's mother fell for him like a ton of bricks. Sid did, too, the minute her baby eyes could make sense of what they saw. But Eddy cared only for the page and slapping down his words—smack, smack, smack—that typewriter of his made one hell of a racket.

He was gone, of course. Lung cancer got him. Sid's mother was in the ground, too. Poor thing lost her marbles early on as these things go, and the money Eddy left got spent on her care, some fancy-shmancy place in Connecticut where everyone smiled and spoke softly. God, it gave Sid the creeps, so she quit going. Didn't matter. Mumsy was completely clueless by then.

Not all the money went. Sid knew a thing or two about investing. Well, her first husband did.

Billy asked if she'd be wanting a trim. He was new. Sid liked his looks, all long and lanky. Nice hands, of course. That was a must. He talked about his cats. A man who had cats had a good soul. She could picture him eating dinner with her in her comfy kitchen. Until the wine hit bottom and he saw the look in her eye. Then he'd bolt. Or not. The ones that didn't wore thin after a while. Sid didn't have as much patience as she used to.

–No trim, Sid said. Leave it long.

–When was the last time you cut your hair?

–Never.

–For real?

–Only enough to keep from sitting on it.

He took her to the shampoo bowl. He led the way. That was the custom, acting as a guide or escort. Trouble was, she was slow. Damned hip complained with each step. And she saw no need to rush anything anymore. Where had it gotten her, all that rushing? Slow or fast, it all gets you nowhere, at the end of the day.

Billy had heard about Eddy the Plume from the guy that used to work there. Billy was an aspiring writer and loved tales of success. When he mentioned this Sid said as far as she could tell—never having written a word in her life—that the thing to do was just start and not stop until you wrote something somebody wanted to read.

Did her dad tell her that?

No, she figured it out all by herself. Besides, it only made sense, right?

He leaned her back into the bowl. She asked him to please put another towel down to pad her neck a little more.

–I'm a pain in the neck, she said.

–Oh, no you're not. You're absolutely splendid!

–Billy? We're going to get along like a house afire!

She was a sucker for the smallest touch of admiration. She had low self-esteem, always had. Her second husband used it to his advantage. She was going through a period of personal liberation. Not doing the dishes, or cooking, or cleaning, though these tasks fell to the hired help. But up to then she'd supervised, made sure it got done to his standards. When she declared that she wanted a bigger world, one beyond the walls of their home, he told her that world would eat her up. Hadn't it already? Is that why she'd come to him in the first place, weary of the insults and criticisms of husband number one? And there he was, no better. Maybe worse. She threatened to give him the boot. He left on his own. He'd found someone else. Someone mousier. That was his word. He used it affectionately, as a compliment. What woman would want to be mousy? Unless she sought the company of a rat. Which he was.

All the men in her life, married or unmarried, to her or to someone else (she got around there for a while; quite the libertine) had one thing in common: they adored her long, thick hair. When the honey-blonde she was born dulled and threaded with gray, she grieved. On her head youth slipped away. Then it slipped from her body, taking along the last of her vanity. Who was there to look good for anymore? The boys she brought home came out of curiosity. And because she paid them. Yes, paid. There it was. The vulgar transaction. Why not? Men rented women all the time. Sometimes they kept them for a while. Sid didn't keep the boys long. They got restless. She got bored.

Billy asked if the water were too warm.

It was, just a little.

He corrected it. She imagined her hair floating like silky weeds in a lake, disintegrating, becoming the medium it lay in. *I am become you.*

One of Eddy's heroines declared that to a man who'd just raped her. Well, okay, it wasn't actually rape. She consented. With his blade to her throat. Then what did she do? Swore that her heart would always be his. Right.

Sid had taken her share of shoves from dear Eddy. If she interrupted his writing, or talked back, or didn't move fast enough when he wanted her to do something. Mumsy tried to protect her, but she wasn't good at that. What was she good at? Crying. Pleading. Turning cold and steely, even to Sid.

Billy asked how she got her name.

–It's short for Siddhartha.

–Really?

–No. For Sydney, Australia. Before he found his voice, Eddy was a merchant marine. That was his favorite port of call.

–Sounds like quite a character.

–You don't know the half of it!

Well, at least she lived well, once he left the world. She traveled, sometimes with her husbands, sometimes alone, sometimes with her best friend, Joann. Oh, Sid missed Joann. Went down in a two-seater on the side of Mount Shasta. They didn't find the wreckage until spring. Joann knew the score. It was she who told Sid to dump husband number two. Joann's daughter Pat was still around. They hung out. Pat was a lesbian, and Sid found her excellent company. The girl knew her wines, too. They haunted wineries when Pat was between acting jobs. Her roles were always bosomy pals, the one you went to with your troubles. Pat's girlfriend left her last spring, and Pat fell apart over at Sid's place for about a month. Sid told Pat to find a useful occupation, so Pat offered herself to the local animal shelter, but that proved to be grief of another kind, seeing the ones nobody wanted, or rather grief of the same kind, when you got right down to it.

Billy wanted to know if Sid had any autographed copies of her father's books.

–I'm afraid not. I gave them all away to local libraries.

–What a beautiful thing to do!

Billy massaged in the shampoo. It smelled like perfume, only richer, with an overlay of coconut. He took his time. He had good fingers.

Sid burned her father's books in the backyard of her Malibu house, on the stone patio she'd just had installed. It was so new she hadn't even set up her outdoor furniture there yet. She didn't like the idea of burning books—it made her think of the Nazis and that novel by Ray Bradbury—but her rage was stronger than regret. Because she didn't have any gasoline to pour over the pile, though she knew she should have some on hand in case the big one hit and she were mad enough to take her car on the road through the chaos, she used single malt scotch. It was her father's favorite drink, which made it appropriate. He'd bought her the bottle because she never had it when he came to visit, and the reason she didn't have it was because he so seldom came. Even so, its absence the two times he crossed her threshold was enough to make him send her a bottle from a distillery in Scotland. The shipping charge alone would have been huge. She emptied the bottle over the books and threw down a lit match. WHOOSH! She thought for a moment of those cooking shows where someone demonstrates how to ignite alcohol and pour the flaming sauce over something sweet and tasty. The book pile was substantial; the flames rose. Then her dingbat neighbor charged through her yard dragging a hose and screaming, though nothing was in danger, no trees nearby. Afterwards, when Sid offered the woman a drink thinking it was the least she could do, she got a lecture on the evils of just one flying spark. The whole neighborhood could have gone up. Didn't Sid know they were all on a high fire alert?

The next day the gardener looked dolefully at the wet, pulpy black mass, and shoveled it all into a wheelbarrow, then dutifully shoveled it all out again into her yard waste container. He put a bunch of dead vines he'd been meaning to cut on top, so the driver, who was known to snoop to make sure people weren't disposing of prohibited plant materials like invasive ivy, wouldn't know. Sid considered his thoughtfulness and gave him a handsome tip at the holidays.

Billy worked in the conditioner, taking time to really massage her scalp. Oh, it was *heavenly!* What was good sex compared to a skilled scalp massage? She closed her eyes, willing his hand to move down the back of her neck and find that knot on the left side that never loosened. Getting old was a real bitch. Isn't that what Eddy liked to say?

That man was born old. Never had a good word about anything, even when success and money came. If anything, he got nastier. For someone so full of hate, he wrote about romance and love convincingly, and women fell all over him. Mumsy knew, of course, and pretended not to care. Sid didn't know for a long time, and when she did, she cared a lot, so much so that she got in his face about it.

Oh, the things she called him! Such deliciousness. She was what, 24 at the time, 25? And being pursued by a young man who raced cars for a living. It turned out he was after her money, or Eddy's money, to be specific, and how Eddy learned of that Sid still didn't know. But he yelled right back at her, calling her a moron, an idiot, a fool who'd never be worth anything to any man except her bank account. Then he said she didn't know anything about being a woman, a real woman, because she took after her mother, and just look at that bag of bitter demands!

Sid swung at him. Yes, she did. And missed. Old Eddy was fast on his feet. He got her by the hair and dragged her out of the room. He pulled so hard that she had a huge lump on her scalp for weeks. Not long after, he wrote a novel about a young woman who escapes being scalped by Indians in the wild west by agreeing to marry the chief's son. Sid never entered Eddy's study again.

When her mother began to lose it, Sid looked for places to put her. There were wonderful facilities in Southern California, but Sid wanted Mumsy as far away from Eddy as possible, hence the opposite coast. Which also meant being away from her, alas. Sid and husband number one lived in Topanga Canyon after the Tate-Manson murders, and their tenure there was shadowed by terror every time they heard a car in the driveway. Husband number two was a director of B films and had a place in Malibu, the place Sid still had, so when Eddy's lungs put him in hospice, his house in La Jolla sat empty. And sat and sat. He wanted Sid to sell it for him. There was a woman he wanted to give the proceeds to. Sid didn't budge. Eddy met his maker, and the same day Sid listed the house. She sold for fifty grand under asking because it needed new floors and kitchen cabinets. Still, she cleared a bundle.

She helped Pat get through school with that money; she helped Joann buy a house. She'd given a grand here and there to countless boy toys whose tales of woe moved her tender heart. She bought a car for one; retired student loans for another; even paid to spay the cat of one sullen, soulful waiter she picked up in a Mexican place in Tarzana where she went after getting her teeth cleaned.

Billy rinsed out the conditioner, helped her sit up, gently wrapped a towel around her hair, and led her back to his station. He was describing his roommate's habit of never doing her dishes, or taking out the trash, and the racket made by the bird she kept in a cage she never cleaned. Billy wished the roommate and the bird would take flight. Then he chuckled at his clever words.

–Where do you live? Sid asked.

–Santa Monica, but I used to live in Venice.

–Pricey hoods.

–Show me a place in LA County that's a bargain.

–True.

Sid said she'd be looking for a tenant to occupy her guest house after the first of the year, if Billy were interested. He asked where that might be, and when she said Malibu, she could see in his eyes what fun it would be to live on the beach.

–Kinda far from work, though, he said.

–I'm sure there are salons there you could hit up.

–Then why don't you go to them?

–Touché.

Billy combed her hair with a plastic comb whose teeth were thick and wide. Now that she'd made her offer, his hands were less gentle, as if he were suddenly in a hurry. He asked if she wanted him to clean up the ends, or if he could just blow her dry.

Sid stared at her reflection. She looked like her father, though less as she'd gotten older, as if the sorrow he'd caused her had slowly rearranged her face. Why not let the transformation continue?

–Cut it, she said.

–How short?

She brought her hand to her chin.

–Are you sure?

–You're not in a hurry, are you?

–Of course not.

He began taking a bit at a time, then larger chunks. Sid's hair lay in silver arcs on the tile floor. She'd never appreciated how it sparkled. She wanted to lift in her hands, now that it wasn't hers anymore, and feel it the way others had always felt it.

But why?

It was just just hair.

Billy kept working. He leaned, came in close, stood back to assess, then cut some more. He was really into it now.

Her head felt as light as her heart.

mavis muldoon

a novella

Kenny, Food Mart's night manager, noticed her first. She was sitting in a lawn chair on the raised bed that divided the customer parking lot. He thought she had probably come to sell something, or gather signatures on a petition, both of which required approval. He took a pair of binoculars the guy before him had left behind when he got fired for being drunk on the job and looked at her up close. Though she had her back to him, he could tell she was old from the way her shoulders slumped. He felt a twinge of sadness as he remembered his own mother, who had passed four years before.

It was almost seven in the morning, and Kenny was getting ready to leave. Jan, whose shift was about to start, called to say she had car trouble. Yes, she knew it was the second time that month. She thought replacing the battery would have done the trick. Her hubby said it was probably the alternator, though he couldn't say for sure.

The office Kenny shared with the other two managers—Clyde covered the swing shirt—was upstairs, next to the employee locker room. It had one large window that was seldom washed. In the winter, the effect was cozy. In summer, which it was then, it was depressing.

The only customers that time of day came into the attached Starbuck's to sit with the paper and a fresh scone. Kenny realized he could do with one, himself. But first he had to find out what the old lady was doing out there, among the creeping Jenny that the landscaping company insisted was a good product.

The air was stale from the fires in Spokane. Olympia was on the other side of the state, but smoke drifted far. Its toxic power was

114

relentless. Yellow skies weren't his thing. And it was funny that he realized that, because the old lady was wearing yellow nail polish.

"Good morning!" he called.

"Good morning."

"Can I help you with anything?"

"Not unless you can turn back the hands of time."

Her wide straw sunhat concealed her face. She tilted her head back and looked up at him. Her skin was a marvel of line and creases. Her blue eyes were clear, arresting, probing.

He asked if she were waiting for someone.

"Only a higher power," she said.

"Okay. Well, I wonder if you'd like to come inside. Is there someone I could call for you? Someone who could give you a lift?"

"I don't need a lift. My bicycle is right over there." She indicated a green bike, leaning up against the brick wall of the store. He wondered how she'd managed to transport her folding chair on it, then realized the chair belonged to the store, taken from the patio where customers who'd just gotten coffee could sit and drink it.

"Okay. Well, just how long do you intend to sit here?" he asked.

"Until it's time to go."

"Look, Miss – Mrs...."

"Mavis Muldoon."

She extended her hand for him to shake. He did. Her grip was tight and firm.

Kenny scratched the back of his head. A car pulled into the lot. The driver, a young mother with a whining toddler, got out. She was a regular at his son's Little League games. Her boy was 11 or 12. The toddler was probably no more than two. That was a big spacing between children. An accident, probably.

Mavis picked up a book of crossword puzzles and a pencil, both of which had been in her lap. He had been dismissed.

He went inside. He called home to say he was going to be late. He went right into voice mail. His wife must be on the phone. She was always on the phone to her sister, or her mother, or her cousin, all of whom lived out-of-state.

Finally, Jan showed up. She was a stern, heavy-set woman, and he didn't ask how she'd managed things with her car. She huffed her way around the office, as she put her coffee cup on the desk, where he was still sitting. He'd been dismissed a second time.

He asked her if she'd seen the old lady in the parking lot.

Yes, she had.

What did she think they should do about her?

"Beats me. Leave her be, I reckon."

"I don't think she should just be allowed to stay there."

"So, call the cops," she said.

He couldn't do that. She was just a nice, strange old lady.

"Then quit worrying about it, and go home," she said.

Around nine, one of the cashiers tracked down Jan to say that a customer had mentioned an old lady sitting in the parking lot. Jan said she knew all about her. The customer had asked if she were all right, if she needed help, and was told everything was fine, *hunky-dory*, in the old lady's own words.

On her morning break, Jan went out to talk to Mavis. When Mavis noticed her, she removed her earbuds. She'd been listening to a podcast on her iPod about the shrinking polar ice caps. She hadn't been able to do the puzzle after all, because she'd left her reading glasses at home.

"You figuring on sitting here all day?" Jan asked her.

"Only until nature calls. Which, since I gave up diuretics, won't be for a little bit, yet. I've got the bladder of a whale."

"I see."

Jan scratched her head.

"I could do with a sandwich, though. Or, better yet, a cookie," Mavis said.

"Yeah?"

"Forgot to bring a snack. Must be going senile."

"You've done this before?"

"Rest awhile in public? Sure."

"But, why?"

"To sit and watch the world go by."

Jan thought a minute. She saw no harm. She went into the store, then down the cookie aisle, chose a package of Chips Ahoy, stood in line to pay, got a curious look from the cashier, and returned to Mavis.

Mavis was delighted, though she could, in good conscience, only help herself to two or three. She handed the bag back to Jan. Jan ate a few cookies, herself.

Just after ten, a group of kids in bright orange tee-shirts bearing the name Westside Day Camp, led by two women, also in orange tee-shirts, poured out of a van and headed for the store. They passed right in front of Mavis, who greeted each one in turn. A little girl stopped and stared at her.

"What are you doing?" she asked.

"Sitting."

"Why?"

"I'm too old to stand."

"How old are you?"

"80."

"I'm seven."

The girl was retrieved by one of the women, who asked Mavis if she were all right.

"Right as rain. Which we could surely use." She looked up at the sky.

"My brother's a firefighter over there. He's says it's been pretty brutal," the woman said.

"May the universe protect him."

The woman nodded. She took the girl and left.

Jan returned a little later and told her customers were starting to ask questions. They didn't know what she was doing there. They thought she might be homeless.

"I most certainly am not. I live with my granddaughter," Mavis said.

"Yeah? What's her number?"

Mavis took out her cell phone from the backpack at her feet and handed it to Jan. She said if she pulled up her contacts list and pressed the first one, she'd be sitting pretty.

The granddaughter answered on the fourth ring. Jan explained the situation.

"Can't you just deal with it?" the granddaughter asked.

"That's why I'm calling you."

"Look, I've got my hands full here. The dog just puked all over the dining room rug, so if you don't mind, you'll have to manage her, yourself."

The granddaughter hung up.

Jan handed the phone back to Mavis.

"Got an earful, didn't you?" Mavis asked.

"Pretty much."

Jan went back inside. She had an employee meeting in a few minutes and didn't have time for this nonsense.

When Mavis came inside to use the restroom, no one noticed her. When she stood a long time, reviewing the greeting cards on offer in Aisle 2, no one noticed her. She bought three cards. Two featured pugs wearing fancy hats. The third was a hand-drawn seascape. Mavis collected cards and wrote words to keep herself going through bad times, of which there seemed to be an increasing number. She was on her way out. Not dying, exactly, just changing. Morphing, in preparation. She believed that her end would be marked by a great transformation. She would become a bird and take flight. Her motivational lines, always in pencil, said things like *You'll be above it all in the end* and *You'll have the best nest yet.* She sometimes wished she'd found a way to make money inspiring others with her unique understanding of metaphysics. The cards were her legacy to her granddaughter, but her granddaughter had no interest in them.

A homeless man had helped himself to her chair in her absence. She ordered him out of it. He complied. As he rose, an earthy, rotten smell rose with him. He sat on the ground, cross-legged and displayed his sign, hand-written on cardboard, *Jesus Saves.*

Mavis told him she'd been raised a Baptist, and that words of the Lord had taken years to fade from her tongue. She didn't believe in a Christian deity. She never had.

He said people responded to a pious plea.

"Not in this town. They're all atheists," she said.

"Then they'll take pity on me for my blighted ignorance," he said.

Mavis complimented him on his elevated manner of speech. He said he'd once been a college man and was an avid reader still. He then volunteered more of his personal history. He'd worked as a commercial fisherman in Alaska until he was injured on the job. Alone, and far from home, he despaired. The Worker's Compensation money ran out faster than it should have, since he turned to drink. Struggling to stay sober and failing, he couldn't find gainful employment. He made his way back to Washington State, where he'd been now for the better part of two years. He stopped drinking, but the despair remained.

"The universe can have a blue tinge," Mavis said.

A teenager walked by and tossed a quarter into the overturned baseball cap in front of where the man sat. He looked at it bleakly. He asked what Mavis was doing there, if she too, were homeless.

"Sometimes I wish I were. The house I live in is not a peaceful place," she said. She told him she was a widow. Her son was gone. When her granddaughter started a family, she moved in to help. Sometimes the past pulled hard. It was easy to feel cut off from things, lost even. That's when she looked up at the night sky. The stars fixed everything.

"I remember that's where I come from, and what I'm made of. I never feel alone then," she said.

But why was she sitting there?

"I'm bird watching."

The man looked at her sharply. She looked back. Dirt and misery made him appear older than he was. His eyes were youthful, though wary.

But why *there*, in a parking lot?

"Look." Mavis pointed to a stand of Douglass firs at the far end. The bicker of stellar jays reached them clearly.

"Some say smoke muffles noise, but I disagree," Mavis said.

The man sighed. He said he was hungry. Mavis asked when he'd last eaten. He said the evening before, he thought. Maybe midday yesterday.

She took a five-dollar bill out of her wallet and handed it to him. She told him to go inside and get something.

"They don't like it when I go in there," he said.

"Too bad."

He took the money and got to his feet.

"Actually, I'm in the mood for burger," he said, gazing across the street at a McDonald's.

"Enjoy," Mavis said.

"Can I leave my backpack here?"

"Sure. I'm not going anywhere."

"Katy might want to come out."

"Katy?"

"My ferret."

The pack wasn't zipped all the way closed, and at the mention of her name, the pack wriggled. The man pulled the zipper to one side, and Katy's head emerged. She looked at the man with love. Then she did the same to Mavis.

Katy wore a harness attached to a leash. The man tied the leash around the slender tree that shaded them.

"Has she eaten?" Mavis asked.

"This morning."

"What do you feed her?"

"Kitten food."

Mavis considered that with limited means, keeping Katy's stomach full was no small feat.

The man said his backpack had a bottle of water and a small plastic dish if Katy got thirsty. He scratched Katy on the head and walked slowly across the lot. Katy strained at the end of leash, watching him go. Mavis told her it was all right; he wouldn't be gone long.

But he was. In fact, after over an hour, he hadn't returned. Just needed to lighten his load, she thought. Well, there was something to be said for that.

Katy had a couple of laps of the water Mavis gave her. She was drawing attention from customers. The cap the man had left behind now held over ten dollars. Mavis had kept track of the coins and bills being deposited. She put the money in his backpack, removed her straw hat, and tried on the cap. It fit. Then she removed it and inspected it closely. It wouldn't do to bring home lice. She put the cap back on. She looked at Katy, who was lying all curled up. If her owner didn't return, Mavis would take her. They'd have to keep her away from the dog, though the dog wasn't much of a threat. Norma was a miniature Chihuahua and weighed all of six pounds. Katy could give her a run for her money. Mavis enjoyed the image of Katy giving chase.

The man came back across the parking lot. His gait was off. It took him several minutes to reach Mavis. He looked down at her, and said nothing of her wearing his cap. He sat down hard next to Mavis' discarded hat. He stroked Katy's head. He smelled of cheap beer, a drink Mavis used to turn to years before.

"Won't do you as much good as a burger would have," Mavis said.

"I'm sorry."

"Don't apologize."

"I'm not off the booze."

"Clearly."

"It helps."

"Until it doesn't."

He cried. Mavis told him to stop. He kept on. She gave him some Kleenex from her backpack. He blew his nose and put the Kleenex in his pocket.

A few minutes later, Mavis' granddaughter pulled up in her Mercedes SUV. She parked about twenty feet away, and marched over, her face etched with rage.

"Hello Isabelle," Mavis said.

"Why aren't you answering your phone?"

Mavis pulled out her phone and looked at it.

"Must have put it on 'silent,'" she said.

"Give it to me." Isabelle took the phone and pressed something on its side.

"Here," she said. She put the phone in Mavis' hand.

Isabelle stopped glaring. Her face showed a blend of relief and annoyance.

"God knows I'm used to it by now, wandering off the way you do," she said.

"You knew where I was."

"Obviously."

The man looked up, and focused.

"I know you," he said.

Isabelle stared at him.

"My god, Jackie Crew," she said.

"Isabelle Muldoon," Jackie said.

"Tatum."

"You married that guy?"

"I did."

Isabelle was a pretty woman—as pretty as her name, Mavis used to tell her when she was small. Her blonde hair was gently graying, now at 35. Looking at her made Mavis remember herself at that age, and how much less she had to work with than Isabelle had. Mavis always tried to take things in stride, then and now. Isabelle was angry a lot, often for days on end.

Isabelle asked Jackie what he'd been up to, since high school. Jackie gave her a thumbnail sketch. Isabelle nodded. She bent down and scratched Katy's head.

"Is everything all right at home?" Mavis asked Isabelle.

"Brian's taking another nap. Tyler's playing a video game. The dog quit puking. I did four loads of laundry then said to hell with it."

"What's wrong with Norma?"

"Who knows? Ate something she shouldn't have, most likely."

"Is she lethargic?"

"Got plenty of energy to hurl all over the place. Seriously, she's fine."

"What kind of dog?" Jackie asked.

"Miniature Chihuahua."

Jackie said his neighbor in Alaska had one of those.

Isabelle said she had some shopping to do and would swing back on her way out. Was there anything she could pick up for either of them? Mavis couldn't think of anything. Jackie couldn't, either.

When they were alone, Jackie said, "Man, life is weird."

"You got that right."

Mavis said she wished Isabelle wouldn't worry about her so much. She could take care of herself. She once hitchhiked all the way down to California. That was in 1961, when she was 22. It was an odd thing to do for a woman at that time. Reckless, many thought. She was running away from her husband. They'd been married about six months then, and she was sure she'd made a terrible mistake. Glen was a decent guy, and they patched up their problems, though it took some doing. It always does though, doesn't it? Hearts don't come together as easily as bodies do, and she hoped Jackie didn't think she was being indiscreet here. She took him to be a man of the world. Anyhow, she threw what she owned into a suitcase and got her thumb out.

"Wow," Jackie said.

She knew there was a good chance she would come to harm, but she didn't. She rode with truckers, a family, a bus full of nuns. The face of one, Sister Eleanor, came back to her still. It was a plain face, unremarkable, as she supposed a nun's face should be, but the eyes were alive with something Mavis couldn't understand. Not faith exactly, but a passion for life that seemed inconsistent with spending one's time here on earth in prayer and acts of devotion.

When she got to San Francisco she found a place to live. She had a little money of her own, another odd thing for women in those days. The other girls in the rooming house were a blend of lost souls, mavericks like her—at least, that's how she liked to think of herself—and do-gooders, you know, charity minded people, givers of all kinds. Teachers, nurses, the ones who held everything together. Before she got married, Mavis worked as a bank teller, and she thought she might be willing to do that again. Anything was better than running through her money and dodging another long-distance phone call from Glen. See, she'd told him where she was, because it was only right that he know. He called about twice a week, and when Mavis added up the cost of all that phone time, he could have paid for a trip down to get her himself. Because that's what she wanted him to do, come down and get her. Not send her the money to come home, not beg over the phone. She wanted him there, at her door, saying okay, she'd had her fun and proved her point, but now it was time to be a wife again.

"And what *was* your point?" Jackie asked.

"That he didn't own me."

She got a job fast enough. She was a nice-looking young woman, and that was very important to people back then, not like now, when you can look like anything at all and still greet the public. And she was very good with figures. So, she stood behind the counter all day, taking money, giving money, making small talk. The customers liked her. She liked her little room, in the house with the other girls. She even learned to like the foggy summer mornings there, in the city by the bay.

One day a woman came to her counter, an old woman, maybe as old as Mavis was now, and handed her a wad of money. She wanted to put it in the bank. She'd had it in her house for too long, she was afraid it was going to get stolen. Mavis asked her to fill out a card with her name and address, and the old woman said she didn't have time for all that. Mavis said it was a requirement of the bank. They had to know for whom they were depositing money. So the old lady took the card and the pencil Mavis gave her and wrote out her name in a wobbly scrawl.

Leonora Blake, her name was. She'd lived in San Francisco all her life. She remembered the earthquake and the fire that followed in 1906. She supposed that was where her drive to save money came from. She gave the card to Mavis, then the money. Mavis counted out the bills. There was over six thousand dollars. The old lady looked at Mavis, as if trying to see inside her, and Mavis just kept smiling and filling out the deposit book. Then the old lady said Mavis should just keep the money. She no longer needed it. She knew her time was nigh, and she had no family to share it with. Mavis said she couldn't possibly. She said anything that came across that counter was the property of the bank. The old lady asked Mavis when she had her next break. Mavis said she took lunch in about another hour and a half. The old lady said she would go get a cup of coffee at the diner on the corner and that Mavis should meet her there. She wanted Mavis to know she was going to try to persuade her to accept her gift, but for the moment, she'd take the money back. Mavis gave it to her. She put the bills back in her purse and went on her way.

Naturally, Mavis had a hard time concentrating after that. Time dragged as it had never dragged before. Finally, she was free to go. The day was clear, the mist all gone. She could still recall the sound of her high-heels slamming the pavement. She got to the diner. The place was packed, and the old lady was nowhere. Mavis even checked in the bathroom. She asked one waitress if she'd seen her, then she asked another, even the cook behind the counter. No one had. Mavis went into a phone booth and looked in the phone book. There was no Leonora Blake listed. Had she imagined the whole thing? Back at work, on an empty stomach that could have used the lunch she'd skipped, Mavis looked at the card the old lady had filled out. It was still there. She hadn't dreamed it.

"I learned then that rules are all well and good, but when opportunity knocks, it's okay to throw the rules out the window," Mavis said.

Jackie's snores were regular and deep. Mavis was tempted to nudge him with her foot, then thought there was no reason to treat him harshly. The man was drunk and undernourished. No wonder he fell asleep.

Isabelle returned. She looked down at Jackie's prone figure on the grass. She asked Mavis if she were ready to come home.

"No."

"So, you're just going to sit here all day?"

"And into the night, most likely."

Isabelle sighed. "Don't overstay your welcome. I don't want a call from the sheriff, too."

"I don't think that will be a problem."

Not long after Isabelle left, a teen-aged girl carrying a long stick walked up and asked Mavis what she was doing, sitting there.

"I'm waiting for my friend here to wake up," Mavis said. The girl looked at Jackie.

"Is he your son?" she asked.

"No."

"Grandson?"

"No. Not kin at all.

The girl poked Jackie's leg with one end of the stick. Mavis told her to leave him be.

The girl went on standing there. She twirled her hair. Mavis decided she was younger than she'd first thought, maybe no more than 13.

"And what's your story?" Mavis asked.

"I don't want to go home."

"Why not?"

The girl twirled her hair some more and shrugged.

"Where are you supposed to be right now?" Mavis asked her.

"On my way back."

The girl said her mother told her to go to the store and get ice cream. Her father loved ice cream when he came home from work. Her mother realized they didn't have any.

"Why didn't your mother go get it, herself?"

"She's not feeling well."

"What ails her?"

Again, the girl shrugged.

Mavis said her mother was going to be worried about her, if she didn't get going soon.

"I'll say I couldn't decide on a flavor," the girl said.

"He doesn't have a favorite?"

"Chocolate. I'll say they didn't have any."

"That's only going to buy you so much time."

"I know."

The girl sat down on the grass and sighed. Her shirt was soiled, and there was dirt under her fingernails.

"How long has your mother been sick?" Mavis asked.

"She's not sick."

"You said she wasn't feeling well."

"She's tired."

Mavis asked if there were any brothers and sisters. The girl said two of each.

No wonder she's tired, Mavis thought.

"And you're the oldest?" Mavis asked.

"Yes."

"How did you get that shiner?"

"Ran into a door."

Mavis asked the girl to tell her her name.

"Leslie."

"That's an uncommon name these days."

Leslie shrugged. Cars came and went. Mavis didn't know the time, but she reckoned from the angle of the sun that it was getting on towards one o'clock.

Leslie looked at Jackie and asked what his problem was.

"Drunk," Mavis said.

Leslie nodded. She looked at Katy and asked if she could pet her. Mavis said sure.

Leslie grabbed Katy by the back of the neck. Katy struggled and twisted in her clutch.

"Hey, now. That's no way to handle an animal," Mavis said. She ordered Leslie to give Katy to her, which she did. Mavis held Katy closely to her for a moment, then set her on the ground where she emptied her bladder. She sniffed suspiciously at the puddle as it soaked into the dry ground, then crawled into the backpack.

Leslie's eyes filled with tears. "I'm sorry," she said.

"You can't go around hurting animals. Or people. Or anything, really."

Leslie broke down. Mavis gave her some Kleenex and told her to blow her nose. After a moment, Leslie calmed.

"I'm going to call someone who will come and talk to you. They're going to ask you about your family, what goes on at home. I don't want you to be scared," Mavis said.

"You mean CPS?"

"How do you know about them?"

A teacher at school, Leslie said. A lady came out to their house and looked around the place. She talked to Leslie's mother. Leslie's father wasn't home.

"Then what happened?" Mavis asked.

"Nothing."

Leslie said she had to go. Mavis wanted to give her her phone number and realized she didn't know it. Why would she, when she never called it? She handed the phone to Leslie.

"Can you tell what this number is?" Mavis asked her.

"I'll send myself a text. Then I'll have it."

Leslie pulled her own phone out of her pocket to verify that the text had been received. The phone had a pink sparkly case. Leslie put it away, and gave Mavis back her phone. Mavis said she could call her anytime she wanted, anytime she didn't feel safe at home.

"I'm sorry I hurt the cat," Leslie said.

"It's a ferret."

"Oh."

Leslie walked off across the parking lot with her stick, turned the corner, and disappeared.

Jackie stirred and sat up. He announced that he was going into the store to use the restroom. After that he should probably get going. Mavis said it had been a pleasure to meet him.

"You, too." He stood and brushed off his pants.

He looked at his cap on Mavis' head. She took it off and gave it to him. She asked him to hand her the straw hat on the ground. He did. She put it on. He said to tell Isabelle it had been really great seeing her again.

"I will."

He hoisted his pack onto his back. Katy wriggled around inside it, then was still.

After he'd gone, Mavis thought about Leslie. She was afraid she'd end up like Jackie. Trauma did bad things to people. It hardened their hearts and destroyed their will. She shouldn't have let her leave. She should call CPS now. Her name might ring a bell. But with no last name, it would take an eager clerk to cross-reference their records. She could give them Leslie's number. There'd be a record of it in her phone. They could track her address from it, couldn't they?

"Oh, bother," Mavis said. The whole thing seemed terribly complicated, all of a sudden. She'd ponder it some more, then run it by Isabelle when she got home. Isabelle could be awfully sensible when she tried.

The eastern sky thickened. Mavis felt cold, thinking about the fire. She'd grown up in Montana. The mountains went up one summer when she was eight. All the men in her town fought the flames. Not all of them came back. The ones who did had blackened faces, streaked with sweat. Her family had to leave home more than once over the years when the fire rolled towards town. Now, with global warming, fires were more frequent. Hurricanes, too. Too many people on the planet, making too much carbon dioxide. People would become extinct, if they weren't careful. And every good thing they'd achieved would vanish along with them.

But what had they achieved? History was full of the effort to eradicate disease, poverty, prejudice, and war. That would never happen until things got more equal. Too much money in too few hands, Glen used to say. He hated the haves because he was always a have-not.

Money was a strange thing, Mavis thought. Everyone wanted it. No one ever seemed to have enough. After losing out on the generous gift from Lenore Blake, Mavis looked upon money with suspicion. It got people into trouble. Glen was a car mechanic. He worried about money all the time—despite the number of expensive phone calls he made when she was out-of-state. He hated paying rent and wanted to buy a house, but it was so hard to save. His spirits suffered. He didn't see the point in anything. His brother owned land in the Skagit Valley, the family farm Glen had fled only a few years before. The parents were dead by then, and the brother said to move up there and help him run the place. So, they did. They made a living selling wool. Mavis learned how to dye yarn and weave. She got pretty good. The other people in the valley, taken with the counter-cultural spirit of the times, adopted a barter system. People moved into the house then out again on a loose, rotating basis. Glen's brother welcomed them all. They grew marijuana and smoked it every day. The police didn't bother them until a runaway showed up. How they tracked her to the farm, no one knew. Everyone got rounded up and spent the night in jail. Mavis had just become pregnant. She had such bad morning sickness they let her go early, before the hearing. Glen was changed by his run-in with the law. His disdain for money made him see that if he'd had some, he probably wouldn't have been arrested in the first place. They left the farm, went back to Snohomish, north of Seattle, where he got a job in another garage. Mavis went on weaving and selling her work at fairs. The baby was born. She named him Franklin.

It made her sad, to think his name. He died in a plane crash just after Isabelle came along. He'd been working on getting his pilot's license, and he went up alone for the first time. Who knew what happened? There had been no mechanical failure; the weather clear as a bell. Maybe he'd wanted to do himself in, and this possibility haunted Mavis to that day. He'd never been a happy person, though he learned to mask it well. Mavis often saw through his good cheer, yet was unable to remedy anything, unable to really take hold of his soul. Isabelle's mother fell apart and couldn't take care of a small child. Glen didn't want to raise her, but Mavis put her foot down and said he could think of her as the daughter they never had. Glen wasn't mean to Isabelle, but he wasn't interested in her either. Maybe she reminded him too much of Franklin, and the grief that never faded. Over the next few years Isabelle's mother, Janice, came and went. She remarried and wanted Isabelle to come live with her. That made Mavis unhappy, but she knew it was the right thing. Janice was in Michigan, a long way from Western Washington. Packing Isabelle's things and getting her ready to go was heartbreaking. Mavis bore that grief alone, because Glen took himself off fishing. Mavis realized that he too would miss Isabelle. He just didn't want to show it.

In the meantime, it took eight-year-old Isabelle all of two months to decide she couldn't stand her new living situation. She got Mavis on the phone nightly, pleading her case. Janice wasn't much of a mother, despite wanting her daughter with her. She liked to party into the night. The husband liked to party even more. He took a swing at Isabelle, something Mavis learned about only after Isabelle came home, riding the bus by herself.

She was easy to raise. She never gave Mavis more resistance than any normal child would. Mavis thought of her more as a friend than a granddaughter. But even the closest friendships can falter, and soon

Isabelle pulled into herself, became secretive. In her teens and twenties Isabelle kept her distance. Franklin was always on Mavis' mind. Such hard, lonely years. She collected cats to keep love alive. Glen hated cats and barely tolerated them. He and Mavis lived separate lives. She knew there were other women and tried not to care. Glen dropped dead in the middle of a brake job. He was 62.

Isabelle married and had a child. She had trouble managing, just as her own mother had. Mavis said she'd move in and take charge. Isabelle said she just needed a little help. The husband, Brian, was a software developer for Microsoft. He did well, though he wasn't home much. Isabelle didn't mind his absence. Neither did Mavis. In fact, when he was there, the balance shifted, and she was on the outside, a long-term guest more than a close family member. The child, Tyler, was a delight. Mavis found his open nature refreshing. He was bright, gifted, did well in school. He was now 14, and spent most of his time in front of his laptop, happy in the fantasy world of online gaming. Mavis thought it was a stupid way to spend one's time. He'd been an avid reader, but over the summer, books stayed closed.

Brian left Microsoft years before and struck out on his own. That's when they moved out of Seattle, down to Olympia. Free-lancing didn't keep him as busy as a full-time job, though apparently the income was pretty much the same. He explained to Mavis that even though he brought in fewer dollars, he had little overhead working from home. And no commute. Microsoft looked upon everyone as a profit center and took from his salary his share of building expenses and maintenance. Free time between projects grew. Isabelle didn't like having him home. He'd just turned 40 and was as healthy as a horse. A grown man shouldn't just sit around with nothing to do. Mavis agreed. The house was large and comfortable, but his inactivity could be felt like a silent weight. He didn't help Isabelle around the house. Mavis did what she could, but she wasn't young. She'd been tired lately. Riding the bicycle out here from Isabelle's had exhausted her, though the road was flat, and the distance no more than a mile and a half.

Her other perch points, as she liked to think of them, were closer to home. She particularly liked the bottom bleacher at the high school's athletic field. She went to see the baseball games last spring. No one bothered her, though several people asked which team she was rooting for. She always said the home team, then pointed to a player and said that was her great-grandson. Her comment always made her inwardly cringe, since Tyler wasn't athletic in the least, which made her lying about him, putting him out there on the field, a curious thing. Maybe in her heart she believed a boy should like sports, that it was the natural thing to do. Then she thought of Franklin, with his love of football, lacrosse, field hockey, and being on the track team. All that running was just an attempted escape from the sorrow he was born with, the sorrow she must somehow have given him.

The playground off Dahlia Drive was another favorite place. Over the years she'd seen the cadre of young mothers change. Now there were a lot of young fathers, too, one of whom she struck up a conversation with not long ago. He was a dental technician and his wife was a lobbyist. His job brought in less money, so he was the one to take time off with the baby. He didn't seem to find it any easier being trapped at home with a child than a woman would have. Maybe he found it harder, since people still thought it a strange thing for a man to agree to. The ideas people had about other people usually caused harm, Mavis thought. Better not to form opinions, or to keep them to oneself. But that never worked, did it? Human beings, blessed with the twin swords of speech and thought, couldn't keep quiet about anything. The man's baby was an ordinary creature, yet extraordinary, too, as babies were. Looking at her in the father's arms, Mavis wondered what path her life would have taken if she'd had more children. If Franklin had had a brother or sister in the world to love and guide him, would he have climbed out of the black hole of his depression and found something to live for? Mavis made the mistake of letting her mind wander and sharing its circuit with the man, whose name she never learned. He'd taken it badly, what she said about Franklin. Suicide wasn't an easy topic to think about, let alone talk about. He looked at his sleeping daughter and must have imagined her doing away with herself one day. Mavis apologized for speaking about gloomy things, and he said it was fine, perfectly fine, but he didn't come to the playground again.

She'd posted herself in other places around town, and most people were nice about it, but once, as she roosted in the parking lot behind a restaurant downtown, the dishwasher came out and screamed at her in Spanish. She had no idea what he said to her, but his meaning was clear. She tried to fathom his rage and couldn't. She must have reminded him of someone in his past who'd been bad to him. A teacher maybe. A lot of folks asked her if she'd been a teacher. Sometimes she said yes, and then when asked what grade she taught she raised their eyebrows by lying that she'd been a professor at a college back east. It was a kind of social experiment, wasn't it? To trip people up, make them confront their expectations and assumptions, which in her case were that an old woman sitting in a parking lot couldn't possibly once have walked hallowed halls.

Mavis was thirsty. The water bottle in her backpack was empty. She didn't remember drinking from it and wondered if it had been empty when she took it out of the kitchen panty at home. Isabelle wouldn't have left an empty bottle in the pantry, but Tyler might have. He was inattentive about household matters, as was Brian. Mavis understood Isabelle's frustration with them, but the solution was easy—stop taking care of them and let them fend for themselves. Mavis thought Isabelle had an overdeveloped sense of duty towards others, gotten no doubt from her own useless mother and Glen's cold shoulder. When you need love from someone, and you don't get it, you work extra hard on their behalf. At least until you figure out that you're wasting your time. Then you think of yourself, for a change. Mavis had tried talking about this to Isabelle, and she wouldn't listen. Maybe she wanted to be a martyr, or just didn't know how to avoid it. Mavis could understand that. She martyred herself to Glen, probably to make up for bolting.

Her temporary absence put up a wall nothing could bring down. But maybe if she'd never left, the wall would have been built over something else, or worse, have risen of its own accord. There were marriages like that. She'd known people, all lost to her now, who had been shut out.

Their first neighbor after they left the farm in the Skagit was Lily Blaine. She was older than Mavis, in her thirties then, with three children she never spoke a cross word to. The eldest took a shine to baby Franklin and liked to feed him. Lily's girl was nine, a good age to practice the responsibility that would one day be thrust upon her— Lily's words, not Mavis'. Mavis thought a girl that age should be out tearing up the world with her brothers, who ran wild in the woods until they got hungry, and scampered home like goats to the barn. One day Mavis told the girl to go on and play, that she'd take care of Franklin. The girl said her father wouldn't like her leaving the house. It quickly became clear that Lily's husband, Ralph, believed that a woman's place was in the home. That hardly made him unique. Glen felt the same way, despite the fact that during the months on the farm he saw women doing men's work out in the fields, or in the barn repairing machinery; and men doing women's work, like baking and cooking, often with poor results, like bread that didn't rise, and roasts that were tough as boot leather. Mavis had made peace with staying home. She'd liked working, but not enough to leave the care of little Franklin to someone else, assuming Glen would ever even agree to that.

One day she asked Lily how she felt about it.

"About what?" Lily asked.

"Being a housewife."

As a young woman Lily dreamed of becoming a nurse. Her parents wouldn't pay for school. They thought it was a waste of time. Their argument was simple—Lily was pretty; she'd soon meet a man and marry; and then what would that expensive training be good for? After her children were grown and gone, and assuming her husband didn't mind, she could get a degree then, assuming anyone would want to hire an older woman.

Lily accepted what her parents said because she had no choice. And sure enough, she met Ralph. Things worked out just as they said it would.

Mavis came to see that Lily wouldn't have minded a life spent cooking, cleaning, and raising children if she'd been loved. It was February, the rains fierce and the wind swift. Valentine's Day had been the week before. Mavis asked what Lily and her husband had done to celebrate and she said they didn't do anything. Mavis and Glen didn't do anything, either, but he'd brought her flowers and was shy handing them to her. When Mavis said so, Lily looked stricken for a moment, until she arranged her face into something bland and impenetrable.

Mavis didn't know if Isabelle got what she needed from Brian. They seemed like actors reading from a script. They only talked about certain things—the weather, how Tyler was doing, if the trash needed to go out, when the next consulting job was coming in. Nothing having to do with Isabelle herself was spoken of, at least not when Mavis was present. Mavis used to be good at sensing what lay in the hearts of other people, but she'd grown more detached, and less in touch somehow.

"Glen."

"Ma'am?"

He looked down at her. With the sun behind him, she couldn't see his face. He wore a short-sleeved green shirt and green pants. His name tag said something she couldn't read.

"You're not Glen."

"No Ma'am."

He was rounding up the shopping carts, she realized.

"Do you want to come inside?" he asked.

"Just to powder my nose. Help me up."

Sitting for so long had stiffened her knees. He extended his hand. She took it and pulled hard until she lifted out of the chair. On her feet, she stood taller than he did. Everything spun madly for a moment. She dropped back into the chair.

"On second thought, be a darling and bring me a bottle of water. Here." She opened her wallet and found another five-dollar bill.

He stared at the money, then took it.

He went off across the parking lot, pushing about ten carts all linked together, nose to tail, like elephants in a circus parade.

The shade offered by the tree was a blessing. It was an alder. Its bark was white and strewn with knots.

Like me, she thought, and smiled to herself.

The cart boy came back with a bottle of water and change. Mavis took the water and told him to keep the change. He said he couldn't do that. She suggested he donate it to charity.

"Like what?" he asked.

"Someone will want it. When I'm gone, bet you anything someone else takes my place on this very spot."

"Are you homeless?"

"No. I wish everyone would stop asking me that."

"Sorry."

He left and Mavis had some water. It was so cold that drinking it was hard. She felt it flow all the way down her esophagus. The effect made her shiver. She should have brought a sweater. Her blouse had short-sleeves. Her pants were lightweight, too. Even her ankle socks were meant for a warm day—which it still was, only the warmth was somewhere else just then.

Her phone rang inside her backpack. The ring tone sounded just like a real phone. Brian thought that was the easiest for her to respond to. Tyler had originally chosen something hip hop, but Brian objected. An old lady and hip hop were two concepts he couldn't hold in his mind at the same time. She didn't want the phone in the first place, but Isabelle insisted. Brian said it was for her safety. Then of course she didn't know how to make it work. There weren't any buttons! Push-button phones themselves had been quite a novelty. And decades before that Mavis had stood on a stool in her house, lifted the receiver, turned the crank to send electricity down the line, and waited for the operator to answer. Then you told her the number, and she connected you.

The phone went silent, then rang again. Mavis bent down to exhume it.

"Hello?"

"Gran-Gran?"

"Tyler?"

"Mom says you're hanging out in a parking lot at the store."

"That's the long and short of it."

"You want company? I can come over with my skateboard."

"Wear your helmet, if you do."

"I don't have a helmet."

"Your parents let you ride that thing without one?"

"I guess."

There was a pause. The driver of a passing car held out a dollar bill in Mavis' direction. She shook her head at him.

"People keep trying to give me money," she told Tyler.

"Maybe they think you're panhandling."

"Yeah, well I'm not."

"Okay."

Another pause.

"Mom wants to know when you'll be home."

"When I wear out my welcome."

"Okay."

They said good-bye and hung up.

Mavis realized she wanted to ask Tyler what Isabelle was making for dinner. Cooking was one of the few things Isabelle really loved doing. Last night they'd had stuffed pork chops that were absolutely delicious. Brian hadn't liked his, so he gave one of his chops to Mavis. Mavis told him his taste buds were duds. She'd laughed at that for quite a while, until a strained looked from Isabelle quieted her. What was wrong with a sense of humor? The world needed to laugh instead of cry. It really did.

A soft breeze lifted the branches of the birch tree but did nothing to clear the fire-stained sky. During the forest blazes of her youth, she'd pray that every breath of wind would push away the smoke that concentrated in the valley where she lived. Mavis hadn't been in Montana for over fifty years. She'd gone back to see her mother before she died. The ranch she grew up on was in bad shape, because the hard-eyed woman who kept it going was wasting away in her bed. Mavis' father sat mutely in his chair, trying to keep his pipe lit, while Mavis cleaned and cooked, hung the wash on the line, and kept Franklin quiet. Her mother's sister, Cora, came out from North Dakota to say her good-byes and make arrangements for a funeral. With her mother in the ground, the father's silence deepened. Three weeks later, he was dead, too, found in his favorite chair, his pipe in his lap. Cora and Mavis listed the ranch for sale. They were in a hurry to be free of it and took a low price. The man who bought it tore it down and put up a luxury hotel where rich people from the east came to gaze at the mountains and ride tame tired horses around the fields. Glen was furious that Mavis didn't hold out for more money. She told him where to go. She'd asked him to go out there with her at the time and he said he couldn't get time off work. She was sure his boss would have given him a couple of days for a family emergency. He just didn't want to bother asking.

Her stomach rumbled. She wished she'd asked that lady to leave some cookies with her.

She got to her feet, glad that the world stayed still this time. She slid her arms through the straps of her backpack and walked across the parking lot. It was a new addition, and she still wasn't used to it. She'd always carried a purse and decided the pack would be more efficient for holding her roosting supplies. Except that she had forgotten the most important things—food and water.

She put her earbuds in and fiddled with her iPod, a hand-me-down from Tyler when his father bought him a new, fancier one. With a lot of help from both Tyler and Brian, she was able to subscribe to Spotify and their curated playlists. Her current favorite featured Peter, Paul, and Mary. Also, early Bob Dylan.

She chose a shopping cart and made for the deli counter, humming "If I Had a Hammer." The fried chicken was tempting, so was the vat of macaroni salad. But the potato salad called her name.

"Eat me," she said, and drew more than one curious glance from nearby shoppers. There was a line. Mavis needed to use the bathroom again, so she left her cart where it was and went slowly to the other end of the store. The air conditioning was cold. It was even colder in the Ladies Room. She sat on her hands when she lowered herself onto the toilet seat. She had no use for those inane paper liners you were supposed to use. It was hard to get back up. She gripped the metal bar bolted into the metal stall divider. Her knees protested. The warm water in the sink took a while to come up. While she waited, she watched a woman change her baby's diaper on the fold-down plastic table at the end of the counter. In her day, bathrooms didn't have such things. You didn't change a diaper in public. You certainly never nursed a baby in public, either. Most women back then put the baby on the bottle, but Mavis gave Franklin the breast. Her doctor cautioned that it would make it hard to get pregnant again right away. He was an old fool who assumed she wanted a big family, because that's what women were good for—breeding. Glen didn't like her breastfeeding Franklin. He said a bottle was good enough. Mavis ignored him, but after only two months she did as he wanted and switched over. Formula wasn't cheap, and when he grumbled about that, she lit into him. He sulked. She soothed. She thought to herself that she had two kids, not one.

She returned to the deli counter, enjoying "Blowin' in the Wind". When the clerk asked if she could help her with anything, Mavis removed her earbuds and said she wanted a large tub of potato salad. As the clerk shoved the salad into the tub Mavis asked if there were pickles in it.

The clerk pointed to a small sign listing the ingredients. Mavis couldn't make it out, without her glasses. Rather than ask the clerk to read her the list, she thought if she came across any pickles, she would just pick them out. The clerk handed her the tub.

"Much obliged," Mavis said.

As she stood in the checkout line, she put her earbuds in, and closed her eyes to "Puff The Magic Dragon." She sang that song to Franklin when he was small. She sang it to Isabelle, then to Tyler. Three generations had held her voice in their ears. And it was a good voice, too. High, clear, and sweet. She could thank the choir at the First Baptist Church of Helena for that. Never missed a Sunday—or a chance to give forth. Until she was about 13, the same age as that Leslie, come to think of it, when she up and quit over the verbal abuse of her parents.

The woman in line ahead of her unloaded her cart. Mavis watched oranges roll on the moving belt, followed by a package of paper towels. The song ended. The silence was hard to hear. The next song played. Mavis opened her mouth, and out came the lyrics to "Leavin' on a Jet Plane." She hadn't heard that song in years, and she became her twenty-something self, wishing that she, like the singer of the song, had traveled first and worn the ring second, not the other way around. She thought then—as she did now—that everything would have been different.

There was a firm hand on her arm.

"Ma'am?" the cashier said.

Mavis once again removed her earbuds. She said she didn't need a bag. She asked where the forks were. The clerk pointed to a table by the wall. Mavis put her credit card in the chip reader and removed it when the message on the small screen told her to.

She left the store with a plastic fork in her pocket and the tub of potato salad under her arm. Singing had filled her with soft light. But where she felt chilly only a little while before, the heat of the afternoon sun now flattened her spirits, and she took off her backpack and sank down gratefully into her chair in the cool shade of her new friend, the birch tree.

She dug into the potato salad. It needed salt. There was no way she was going to huff it back across the parking lot and help herself to the small paper packets next to the plastic utensils. She ate a few more forkfuls, enjoying the creamy mayonnaise and the tart taste of white wine vinegar. She left out the vinegar when she made her first batch of potato salad for Glen. She could tell he missed something, but he kept eating. A hungry man was great to have around when you were learning how to cook. Your bad food never went to waste. Their kitchen was a study in yellow. Even the toaster, which had taken some work to find, reminded her of a gleaming egg yolk that had just been slid onto the plate. She'd read in a magazine that a cheerful kitchen was crucial to a happy marriage. She wanted a happy marriage. She had one, for a while. Until the panic set in—looking down the stretch of her life and seeing only what she had then, that yellow kitchen and a husband who declared it was his least favorite color.

Glen never wanted to be a father. She knew that from the beginning. The two of them together with no other focus, no other outlet, nothing else to receive love and be nurtured, felt wrong. She supposed that pulled them apart, more than anything else. Yet he adored Franklin and suffered horribly when his plane went down.

They should have talked about it. They weren't the kind of people who were open about painful feelings. Mavis had found her voice since those days. She was gently critical of the way Brian didn't do his share of the housework, and the hours Tyler spent with a game controller in his hand.

Where were they now, Franklin and Glen? Nowhere. They weren't anywhere. And when she died, Mavis wouldn't be anywhere, either. Some said the dead didn't disappear, but they did. Okay, they might be remembered for a time, that was all fine, but you couldn't say that a pile of bones or a can of ashes meant you were still on earth.

Only the living could make that claim.

The lack of salt in the potato salad really bothered her then. She'd cut back so much, after being told she had high blood pressure. She even lost weight, got some exercise. Hence the bicycle.

She couldn't say what made her glance over at the side of the store where she'd propped her bike. Maybe she sensed it was gone. She hadn't secured it when she went to set up her chair in the shade. That was stupid of her. And what a lousy thing to do, to steal an old woman's bicycle. It was a good one, too. She'd gotten it second-hand from a graduating college student. The girl looked at her skeptically when Mavis asked her how to move the seat higher to accommodate her long legs.

She got out her cell phone and held it at arm's length to read the screen. How the hell had she managed to forget her damned glasses, anyway? She pulled up her contacts list. There were two names besides Isabelle's—Brian and Tyler. She pressed the phone icon under Tyler's name.

Tyler answered after six rings.

"Hi Gran-Gran. I'm sorry I didn't come by. I'm on Level Four of 'Capture the Moon.'"

"Honey, someone took my bike."

"Yeah?"

"I wonder if I should call the police."

"Maybe. But they'll probably never find it."

"Crap."

They paused.

"Gran-Gran?"

"I went in to buy something to eat. I didn't notice if it were there or not. I should have. It didn't occur to me."

"Are you all right?"

"Oh, I suppose. Say, can you bring over the saltshaker from the dining room table?"

"Did you say saltshaker?"

"I did." She explained why she wanted it. Cheerful, cartoonish music played in the background. Then it stopped.

"Uh, hang on," Tyler said. She heard him calling for Isabelle. After a moment Isabelle said, "Grandma?"

"Can you bring me the saltshaker? I got this delicious potato salad from the store, but it's on the bland side. I think everyone's gotten salt-shy. Garlic-shy, too, not that there should be garlic in a potato salad. You know what I mean. I hope."

"You want me to bring you a saltshaker."

"That's the long and short of it. Oh, someone stole my bicycle."

"What? Didn't you use the chain and lock I bought you?"

"Must have left those at home."

Isabelle sighed. She could be heard calling for Brian. Their conversation was audible, but not their words. Then Isabelle came back on the line.

"We're on our way. Don't move," she said.

"Don't forget the salt."

Isabelle hung up. Mavis put her earbuds and iPod away. She didn't want more music just then.

She'd like to kick whoever took her bike. She looked out over the parking lot to see if anyone were riding it around, but that was silly, because who would stick around after taking it? People could be stupid, though. There were those two guys who held up a bank, then went to celebrate two blocks away at a Chucky Cheese where the cops found them knee-deep in a greasy pepperoni pizza. The paper said they were shocked that the cops found them so fast. Idiots!

It was a nice bike, the one Franklin got for his tenth birthday. Fiery red, almost orange. Of course, Glen said it was a stupid color; black was what a boy should have. Mavis found it at a garage sale. It was in great shape, and much less expensive than a brand new one would have been. Glen also didn't like that it was used, but when she told him what she would have had to spend otherwise, he piped down pretty quick.

The bike gave Franklin freedom. He rode and rode, miles from home. They were living back in the Skagit Delta then, where the lanes were wide and flat. But Mavis worried about him out there so long, day after day. She was glad when the winter rains set in. When he was older, he begged for a motorcycle. Glen told him he had to earn the money, himself. He arranged a part-time job for him at the repair shop where he worked. Franklin was good with cars—even better than Glen. He had a real knack for machinery, something innate. He was much less good with people, and with himself. He would get frustrated by something, usually a kid at school, or not doing well playing baseball or football, and he'd rage. He slammed doors, broke things, hurled insults.

One in particular was still very much alive.

"You're nothing, either one of you, but you . . . you're worse. You're his doormat, his punching bag, and you're too stupid to even see!"

Glen lost it. He smacked him around, more than once. Franklin never fought back. Mavis got between them, told Glen to calm down, then tried to talk to Franklin, feel him out, get to the bottom of what drove him so hard, but never had any luck.

So, Franklin saved his money and bought a Harley that was in rough shape. He spent one whole winter rebuilding it in the garage, which ticked Glen off because he couldn't put his truck in there after work. Mavis always parked in the driveway, and she told Glen he could, too. His precious truck wasn't going to melt in the rain. Franklin was a different person, working on that motorcycle. Calm, focused, sometimes optimistic. When the work was done, he only rode the bike once. Mavis asked him why. He said he didn't want to mess it up.

"You rebuilt it to ride it, not look at it," she said. She wasn't angry, just confused. It seemed as if he were afraid of it, or that it didn't really belong to him now that he'd put it back together. After a while he sold it and shared the money with Glen to pay him back for occupying the garage so long. Mavis thought that was all nonsense. The garage belonged to all of them. It was attached to the house they all lived in. She never said so, though. She knew it would be pointless.

She was tired. Riding the bike over here had been so hard! Wasn't it providential that it was gone now? That she'd have to accept a ride home?

That was something her mother would have said. The Lord, working in his mysterious ways. The argument Mavis would make was that it wasn't the Lord, but the universe. They weren't at all the same thing. A lord, any deity, was focused on human beings. The universe wasn't. The Lord as far as Mavis could tell was a pain in the ass who did his best to mess people up.

"That's blasphemous, Mavis."

"Cool it Mom. It's just the truth."

When did she ever tell her mother to cool it? She didn't. But she'd thought it plenty of times.

Her poor mother, a rough woman with a soft name—Della. Della was no fool, but her devotion to God went against the deep, logical way she viewed just about anything else. It was as if she had to give some part of herself over to faith, or to something she couldn't truly understand but still needed to keep close. Over time, Mavis saw that her attachment to the unfathomable was her response to living with Mavis' father, who kept his thoughts to himself. She never seemed to know what he was thinking, but Mavis could always tell. Frustration was shown with pressed lips; joy with a quicker stride across the room; misery by a gaze that went right out the window to the mountain tops in the distance, as if he wished he were there, free of responsibility.

When disaster was averted, if a forest fire came close but didn't harm their ranch for instance, Della thanked God for sparing them. Mavis thought if God wanted to do something, he would have kept the fire from starting in the first place. Della was devoted to her church, but her country ways were too much, even in a rural congregation, and she stopped going as often. She confided to Mavis that she'd overheard an unkind remark about the rubber boots she wore one time. She'd been busy in the barn, ran late, didn't have time to put on better shoes, though she did put on her gingham dress, which she'd pressed the night before. And her hat had a new ribbon, didn't that count for something? Mavis was moved by her mother's hurt feelings, even when she didn't admit to them. She was easier on her after that, if only in her mind.

When Mavis left Montana for Washington State her mother didn't say a word. She packed a lunch to take on the bus—a cheese sandwich and pickle, wrapped in wax paper. Mavis was going to Everett to work as a teller in a bank that also had a branch in Helena. It was a big, national bank, and she was lucky to get the transfer she asked for. She had to get off that ranch. She was tired of driving her father's ancient truck fifteen miles one way to work. She suggested that she find a room in town to save the time and expense, but her mother wouldn't hear of it. A young woman lived at home until she married; hence the wall of silence when her father drove to the bus station.

Mavis carried her mother with her a long time; in some ways, she carried her still. Children were never entirely free of their parents; parents were always tethered to some degree to their children. What was the point of pretending that in matters of blood there was any true independence? Or matters of the heart, truth be told.

Mavis looked at the tub of potato salad in her lap. She ate some more of it, wishing again for salt.

Her phone rang. She hadn't realized she'd dropped it on the ground, but there it was, ringing away. Her lower back, which bothered her all the time, wouldn't let her bend that far. A young couple was just then passing, hand in hand, sullen-faced, as if they didn't really want to be touching each other. Mavis asked if they could give her the phone. The man had a soul patch and a tattoo of a snake around his neck. He looked like a rough character, but his eyes were mournful and watery, like a little boy's. The woman had bad teeth and pitted skin, yet her hair looked soft and Mavis found her pretty. The phone stopped ringing. The man picked it up and examined it. He turned it over. The woman looked at him and shook her head. He gave the phone to Mavis.

"What are you doing out here?" the woman asked her.

"Waiting for my family."

The woman nodded.

"I don't suppose you have any spare change," the man said.

"You're panhandling a panhandler?" Mavis asked.

"No."

"Just kidding. Here." Mavis handed him her wallet from the pack, which was easier to reach, since it sat up against her chair.

The man took the wallet and looked at Mavis.

She told him to open it and take out a five. Or a ten, but she didn't think she had a ten. And she hoped he wasn't getting the idea to take her credit card because she was basically maxed out. Her credit limit was pretty low. That was her granddaughter's doing. The granddaughter held the purse strings. And it was a hefty purse. It would be even heftier if her husband put himself out there a little more. She'd always heard that a consultant had to stay in the game for people to find you, but he did one job, then sat on his rear end for over a month. Doing what, they were never completely sure. He seemed to read and sleep. He said once he was writing something. Mavis assumed he meant creative writing. Whatever.

The man gave her the wallet back. He said he didn't need her money, it was okay. He hoped her family would show up soon. Did she want them to wait with her until then?

"Don't be silly. You've already done enough, giving me my phone and all."

The man and woman left. Mavis peered at the phone. Brian's name and number were displayed under missed calls. The phone rang again.

"Mavis? Listen, Isabelle wanted me to let you know that the dog threw up again and she wants to take her to the vet. So, we're going to do that first, then come over there. Okay?"

"What about my salt?"

"What salt?"

"The salt for the potato salad."

"I don't know what you're talking about."

"Oh, Brian. What else is new?"

Mavis pictured him with his phone to his balding head. He'd be in one of his palm-tree decorated silk shirts—the yellow was his favorite—a pair of shorts that had pockets down the legs so you could go hiking and carry your wallet, keys, and phone, though as far as Mavis knew he didn't hike—and flip-flops. His glasses would be smudged. He never cleaned them. His fingernails were dirty, too. He didn't wear a wedding ring. None of this added up to anything more than a man who lived in his own world.

"I'm sorry," Mavis said.

"For what?"

"That Norma's not feeling well."

"She probably ate something she shouldn't have."

"Dogs do that."

They paused. Mavis heard Tyler calling for Brian.

"I have to go," Brian said.

"Okay."

He hung up.

Mavis considered her options. She could call a cab. People also used Uber these days, but she'd heard bad things about them. She could go on sitting, watching the sky thicken in the east, and accept the lack of salt. The last option was the best, by far.

Brian was depressed, she realized. That's why it was so hard for him to work consistently. Did Isabelle know? She was sharp but burned out. There was something keeping her from what she wanted in life, and it wasn't just Brian. She had too many choices. Things were too easy. Isabelle needed the threat of penury to get her moving.

Mavis was glad Isabelle was putting Norma's welfare above her own. Animals were important. They mattered. People tended to forget that.

A trio of ravens circled in the distance, then landed on the high branches of a Douglas fir. They must think that human beings were awfully stupid, carrying on the way they did. Or maybe, if the ravens were lucky, they didn't think about people at all. But how could they not? The world they lived in had been sullied by men from the time they could stand and throw spears, or even before, if Mavis had to guess. The human race was a horde that every other living thing had to make way for. And there were more and more of them all the time. Sometimes Mavis thought she could hear the earth groan under the weight of those billions of bodies. Too many people needing too many things. Why did people have so many children, anyway? She had one. Isabelle had one. The Chinese government had it right—limit couples to one child. She didn't agree that the government should force women to have an abortion if they went over their quota. She also didn't believe the government should tell a woman not to have an abortion. Who got to say, anyway? Who had the right to tell a woman anything about her body?

"We're not breeding stock, you know," Mavis told the air.

Suddenly, she was tired of sitting there. The afternoon light had crept around the increasingly meager shade. She got up, checked her pack to make sure it had everything she left home with, and carried the chair toward the spot she took it from in the morning. She didn't remember it being so heavy! It was just a simple plastic chair. Flimsy, really. A strong wind would send it off somewhere.

Mavis shivered. How in the world could she be cold, expending effort like this? Maybe she was coming down with something. Maybe there was something going around.

Her knees buckled, and down she went. The asphalt didn't feel hard beneath her. Really, it felt as if she were lying on nothing at all.

It was later. There were lights and sounds, both mechanical and human. People talking. Someone chuckling. Her body felt like lead. Where had all the lightness gone? And that lovely floating sensation?

"She's awake," someone said.

"Grandma?"

"Who's that?"

"Isabelle."

"How's Norma?"

"What? She's fine."

There was a hand in hers. Mavis focused. It was Isabelle all right, looking like she hadn't slept in about two years.

Isabelle told her she'd fainted in the parking lot of the store. The medics were called. They went through her backpack and found her phone. They called each number in her list, but no one's phone rang. Isabelle didn't know why. Maybe that's when they were in the vet's office, and the cell signal was bad. They went on to the store with the saltshaker after dropping Norma at home, but Mavis wasn't there. That's when Isabelle pulled out her phone and saw the message about what happened.

"What *did* happen?" Mavis asked.

"They thought it was your heart, or maybe a stroke, but you were just dehydrated."

"So why can't I remember being brought here? Where is here, anyway? The hospital?"

"Yes. I don't know. They said you were awake and talking."

"What do you know about that."

Mavis realized that Tyler and Brian were in the room, too. She wished they'd brought Norma. Norma would be a great comfort along about now, with her bright shiny eyes and perky little ears. Norma was the easiest one in the whole family to talk to.

Mavis asked Brian and Tyler to wait outside. Isabelle took some money from her wallet and told Brian to find the cafeteria and get themselves something to eat.

When they'd gone Mavis said, "If you have any idea about putting me in a home, you can forget it."

"I'm not thinking any such thing."

"Yes, you are. I can see it in your face."

"I'm just worried."

"No point in worrying. We all have to go sometime. Today just wasn't my time, that's all."

The tape securing the clear plastic tube in her arm itched. She wondered if there were any more potato salad around. She asked Isabelle. Isabelle didn't know what happened to the potato salad, but she could ask the nurse in a minute.

"Oh, don't bother. It's probably spoiled by now, anyway. It was pretty good, though. I'll give it that."

A man in a white coat came in. He looked Japanese. He listened to Mavis breathe with a stethoscope and shined a light in her eyes. Then he took her pulse. He asked how she was feeling.

"Never better."

"Your electrolyte balance was off. You need to drink more fluids. And your blood pressure is high. Your granddaughter said you were previously on medication."

"Yeah. I gave it up. Had to pee all the time."

"I can prescribe something that doesn't make you have to go to the bathroom a lot."

"Wonderful."

The doctor said she was lucky she hadn't hit her head. She'd just crumpled up in a heap.

"Like someone cut the puppet's strings."

"Yes. Something like that."

Mavis asked how long she had to stay there. Not that the bed wasn't comfortable, mind you. It was lovely. It was just that her favorite show was on that night.

The doctor said it shouldn't be too much longer. He'd ordered a visit from a social worker.

"Whatever for?" Mavis asked. She struggled to sit up. Her head throbbed.

The doctor said she seemed fuzzy about her surroundings and wasn't sure why she was at the store.

"Well, I wasn't at the store. I'd been sitting in the parking lot. Under a tree. On some grass. Oh, Isabelle, you tell him."

Isabelle did. The doctor asked her if she thought it a good idea for a woman Mavis' age to sit all day in a parking lot.

"You tell her what to do, and see where it gets you," Isabelle said.

Mavis clapped.

The doctor asked Isabelle if she were going to keep a close eye on Mavis over the next few days. Isabelle said yes, she was. The doctor said he could probably arrange to have the social worker come to the house.

"Forget it," Mavis said.

The doctor said any further episodes of confusion should be reported.

"Fine," Isabelle said.

When he left, Mavis said she didn't appreciate him thinking she was just some dingbat who'd wandered off. Isabelle said it was understandable that he think that. Mavis reminded her she would have been home sooner if her bicycle hadn't gotten stolen, and that she'd said they were coming to get her and then didn't.

"I know, I know," Isabelle said. "Blame it on the dog."

"What's wrong with her, anyway?"

"She ate a bunch of landscaping bark. Didn't agree with her."

"I should say not."

Mavis said Isabelle looked tired. Had she eaten? Isabelle said she hadn't. Mavis told her to go join Tyler and Brian, and then come back when she was ready. It's not like she was going anywhere, right?

At that Isabelle looked alarmed, and Mavis realized that Isabelle thought it possible that Mavis would just get a notion to up and leave. Mavis wished she'd thought of it, herself.

But where would she go now? She just wanted to go home.

Isabelle left. A nurse came in to check on her and closed the curtain that kept people from looking in when she left. Mavis didn't care if they looked or not. She would rather the curtain remained open, and thought she'd call the nurse back, but didn't feel like it. The truth was, she felt awfully worn out by the day's events. She could do with a good night's sleep.

She drifted in and out, waiting for her family to come back. She thought about where she might roost next. Maybe somewhere out-of-town. She'd have to borrow a car. She hadn't renewed her license when the notice came in the mail. She was pretty sure she'd fail the vision test this time around. That could be a problem if she got pulled over. She'd given Isabelle a lot of trouble today. She didn't want to add to it. Now, if she could convince Isabelle to go with her, that might be a different story. But Isabelle wouldn't want to go with her. She hadn't learned the fine art of sitting. Brian had, but Mavis didn't want his company. That was uncharitable, and she felt bad, but only for a moment.

Maybe she'd just do her roosting at home, from now on. The recliner in the living room had a great view of the back yard. It might be nice to watch the season change. Tyler would be back in school soon, and Brian would make himself scarce until the next gig came in, assuming he'd even take it. With her around to keep an eye on things, maybe Isabelle would get out more, find something she liked to do. She said once she'd like to work in a bookstore. Well, fine. Now she could. That girl needed new faces, new voices in her ear. Maybe a new husband, but that was a stretch.

Mavis woke up to the nurse saying she could get dressed now. Mavis asked where her family was. The nurse said they were in the reception area, waiting for her. Did she need help? Did she want her to send her granddaughter back?

"No, I can manage," Mavis said.

Mavis moved slowly. She got into her underpants, wrestled with her bra, pulled on her shirt and pants, then her socks. She slipped into her sneakers and sat back on the bed to tie the laces. She thanked the universe for looking out for her and helping her accept that her life was about to change.

Again.

about the author

Anne Leigh Parrish is the author of *Maggie's Ruse*; *The Amendment*; *Women Within*; *By the Wayside*; *What Is Found, What Is Lost*; *Our Love Could Light The World*; and *All The Roads That Lead From Home*.

about the press

Unsolicited Press was founded in 2012 and is based in Portland, Oregon. The small press publishes fiction, poetry, and creative nonfiction written by award-winning authors.

Learn more at www.unsolicitedpress.com